"What do you want?"

The man who'd fed her and provided her protection and light in a blackout didn't sit across from her. No, this wasn't the man who'd introduced her to such pleasure she still felt the echo of it weeks later. This man... He was a stranger. A cold, calculating, beautiful stranger.

"You."

The blunt announcement doused her in a frigid blast of water, stunning her.

"Excuse me?" she rasped.

He couldn't mean... No. No way. He didn't want her. He had to mean something else. But God, her body was having one hell of a time getting the message. *You.* Heat prickled at the base of her spine, and desire wound through her veins like a molten stream.

"I want you." He leaned forward, his midnight gaze pinning her to her chair. "More specifically, I want you to be in love with me."

* * *

Black Tie Billionaire is part of the Blackout Billionaires series.

Dear Reader,

The blackout that plunges the city of Chicago into darkness claims another couple!

I have a confession to make... I love revenge and blackmail stories. I do! They're my weakness. It's watching the passion of pain and vengeance transform into something softer, more forgiving, more loving and accepting. *Sigh*. And then, of course, there's all that enemies-to-lovers heat between the hero and heroine. Can't deny that!

In *Black Tie Billionaire*, Gideon Knight seizes the opportunity to avenge his family and destroy his enemy. And he uses Shay Neal, his enemy's sister, to do it. But he doesn't count on the woman he's blackmailed to be so fierce, proud and unbreakable. Shay may have submitted to his "arrangement," but she's no man's pawn. They face off in a battle of wills and secrets that may end up with casualties on both sides...or may save them both with the love of a lifetime.

There's drama, retribution, sizzling heat, compassion and the overwhelming healing power of love in this story of family pitted against family. I hope you love Gideon and Shay as much as I do!

Happy reading!

Naima Simone

NAIMA SIMONE

BLACK TIE BILLIONAIRE

Recycling programs
for this product may
not exist in your area.

ISBN-13: 978-1-335-60387-6

Black Tie Billionaire

Copyright © 2019 by Naima Simone

This edition published by arrangement with Harlequin Books S.A.

For questions and comments about the quality of this book,
please contact us at CustomerService@Harlequin.com.

® and TM are trademarks of Harlequin Enterprises Limited or its
corporate affiliates. Trademarks indicated with ® are registered in the
United States Patent and Trademark Office, the Canadian Intellectual
Property Office and in other countries.

Printed in U.S.A.

www.Harlequin.com

USA TODAY bestselling author **Naima Simone**'s love of romance was first stirred by Harlequin books pilfered from her grandmother. Now she spends her days writing sizzling romances with a touch of humor and snark.

She is wife to her own real-life superhero and mother to two awesome kids. They live in perfect, domestically challenged bliss in the Southern United States.

Books by Naima Simone

Harlequin Desire

Blackout Billionaires
The Billionaire's Bargain
Black Tie Billionaire

Visit her Author Profile page at Harlequin.com, or naimasimone.com, for more titles.

You can find Naima Simone on Facebook, along with other Harlequin Desire authors, at Facebook.com/harlequindesireauthors!

To Gary. 143.

One

She was beautiful.

Gideon Knight tuned out the man speaking to him as he studied the petite woman weaving a path through the crowded ballroom. Even wearing the white shirt, black bow tie and dark pants of the waitstaff, she stood out like the brightest jewel among the hundreds of guests at the Du Sable City Gala, the annual event of the Chicago social season, rendering those around her to mere cubic zirconia.

How was it that only *he* noticed the elegant length of her neck, the straight line of her back that tapered at the waist and flowed out in a gentle, sensual swell of hips? How did the other people in the room not ogle the particular way the light from the crystal chandeliers hit her bronze skin, causing it to gleam? How did they not stop and study the graceful stride that wouldn't have been out of place on the most exclusive catwalk?

Had he said beautiful? He meant exquisite.

And he hadn't even seen her face.

Yet.

"Excuse me." Gideon abruptly interrupted the prattling of the older gentleman, not bothering with a polite explanation for walking away.

The other man's surprised sputtering should've dredged up a semblance of regret, especially since Gideon's mother had hammered better manners into him. But just ten years ago this gentleman wouldn't have deigned to acknowledge Gideon's existence. Then he'd been just another penniless, dream-filled, University of Chicago business student. He hadn't been *the* Gideon Knight, cofounder and CEO of KayCee Corp, one of the hottest and most successful start-up companies to hit the market in the last five years. Now that he was a multibillionaire, this businessman, and people of his tax bracket and social sphere, damn near scraped their chins on the floor with all the bowing and kowtowing they directed Gideon's way.

Money and power had that peculiar effect.

Usually, he could dredge up more patience, but he despised events like this high society benefit gala. One thing he'd learned in his grueling battle to breach the inner sanctum zealously guarded by the obscenely wealthy one percent was that a good portion of business deals were landed at dinner tables, country club golf courses and social events like the Du Sable City Gala. So even though attending ranked only slightly higher than shopping with his sister or vacationing in one of Dante's nine levels of hell, he attended.

But for the first time that he could remember, he was distracted from networking. And again, for the first time, he welcomed the disruption.

He wound his way through the tuxedoed and gowned throng, pretending not to hear when his name was called, and uttering a "Pardon me" when more persistent individuals tried to halt him with a touch to his arm. Many articles written about him had mentioned his laser-sharp focus, and at this moment, it was trained on a certain server with black hair swept into a low knot at the back of her head, a body created for the sweetest sin and skin that had his fingertips itching with the need to touch...to caress.

That need—the unprecedented urgency of it—should've been a warning to proceed with caution. And if he'd paused, he might've analyzed why the impulse to approach her, to look into her face, raked at him like a tiger's sharp claws. He might've retreated, or placed distance between him and her. Discipline, control, focus—they were the daily refrains of his life, the blocks upon which he'd built his business, his success. That this unknown woman already threatened all three by just being in the room... Not even his ex-fiancée had stirred this kind of attraction in him. Which only underscored why he should walk away. It boded nothing good.

Yet he followed her with the determination of a predator stalking its unsuspecting prey.

How cliché, but damn, how true. Because every instinct in him growled to capture, cover, take…bite.

She would be his tonight.

As the strength and certainty of the thought echoed inside him, he neared her. Close enough to glimpse the delicate line of her jaw and the vulnerable nape of her neck. To inhale the heady, sensual musk that contained notes of roses, and warmer hints of cedarwood and amber…or maybe almond.

Tonight's mission would be to discover which one.

For yet another time this evening, he murmured, "Excuse me." But in this instance, he wasn't trying to escape someone. No, he wanted to snare her. Keep her.

At least for the next few hours.

Look at me. Turn around and look at me.

The plea rebounded off his skull, and the seconds seemed to slow as she shifted, lifting her head and meeting his gaze.

His gut clenched, desire slamming into him so hard he braced himself against the impact. But it still left him reeling. Left his body tense, hard.

A long fringe of black hair swept over her forehead and dark-rimmed glasses perched on her nose, but neither could hide the strong, regal lines of her face, the sharp cheekbones, the chocolate eyes or the lush siren's call of her mouth.

Damn, that mouth.

He dragged his fascinated gaze away from it with a strength that deserved a gold medal. But nothing, not even God Himself, could cleanse his mind of the acts those curves elicited. Acts that left him throbbing and greedy.

"Did you need a glass of champagne?" she asked, lowering her eyes to the tray she held.

No, keep your eyes on me.

The order rolled up his throat and hovered on his tongue, but he locked it down. Damn, with just a few words uttered in a silk-and-midnight voice, he'd devolved into a caveman.

Once more, a warning to walk away clanged inside him, but—like moments earlier—he ignored it. Nothing else mattered at the moment. Nothing but having that sex-and-sin voice stroke his ears. Having those hands slip under his clothes to caress his skin. And those oval-shaped eyes fixed on him.

"What's your name?" He delivered a question of his own, answering hers by picking up a glass flute full of pale wine.

If he hadn't been studying her so closely, he might've missed the slight stiffening of her shoulders, the minute hesitation before, head still bowed, she said, "I need to continue…"

She shifted away from him, preparing to escape into the crowd.

"Wait." He lifted his arm, instinct guiding him to grasp her elbow to prevent her departure. But at the last moment, he lowered his arm back to his side.

As much as he wanted to discover how she felt under his hand, he refused to touch her without her permission. Rich assholes accosting the waitstaff was as old a story as a boss chasing his secretary around the desk. Even though his palm itched with the lack of contact, he slid his free hand into his front pocket.

The aborted motion seemed to grab her attention. She raised her head, a frown drawing her eyebrows together.

"Gideon Knight," he said, offering her his name. "You have my name. Can I have yours?"

Again, that beat of hesitation. Then, with a small shake of her head, she murmured, "Camille."

"Camille," he repeated, savoring it as if it were one of the rich chocolate desserts that would follow the dinner course. "It's a lovely name. And it fits you."

Her eyes widened, an emotion he would've labeled panic flaring in their depths before she lowered her lashes, hiding her gaze from him. Again. "Thank you, Mr. Knight. If—"

"Gideon," he corrected. "For you, it's Gideon."

Her full lips firmed into a line seconds before she met his stare with one glinting in anger. How insane did it make him that he found the signs of her temper captivating...and sexy as hell?

"No offense, *Mr. Knight*—"

"In my experience, when someone starts a sentence with 'no offense,' they intend to offend," he drawled.

Once more he saw that flicker of anger, and an exhilaration that was usually reserved for fierce business negotiations surged in his chest. The exhilaration meant he was engaging with a worthy opponent.

"I'm going out on a limb and assuming your ego can take the hit," she shot back. Then, as if she realized what she'd snapped—and who she'd snapped at—she winced, briefly squeezing her eyes shut. "I apologize—"

"Oh, don't disappoint me now by turning meek, Camille," he purred, arching an eyebrow.

In a distant corner of his mind, he marveled at who he'd become in this moment. Flirting, teasing, goddamn *purring*—they weren't him. His mouth either didn't know this information or didn't care. "I assure you, I can take it," he added.

Take whatever she wanted to give him, whether it was her gaze, her conversation or more. And God, he hungered for the *more*. Greedy bastard that he was, he'd claim whatever she chose to dole out.

"Mr. Knight," she began, defiance clipping his name, "I don't know if approaching the staff and toying with them is one of your usual forms of entertainment. But since you've invited me not to be *meek*, let me tell you this might be a game to you, but the waitstaff aren't toys to alleviate your boredom. This is a livelihood for workers who depend on a paycheck and not getting fired for fraternizing with the guests."

Shock vibrated through him like a plucked chord on his favorite Martin D-45 acoustic guitar.

Shock and…delight.

Other than his mother and family, no one had the balls to speak to him like she had, much less reprimand him. Excitement—something he hadn't experienced in so long he couldn't remember the last occurrence—tripped and stumbled down his spine.

"I don't play games," he said. "They're a waste of

time. Why be coy when being honest achieves the goal faster?"

"And what's your goal here, Mr. Knight?" she challenged, not hiding her sneer.

If she understood how his pulse jumped and his body throbbed every time she stated "Mr. Knight" with a haughtiness worthy of royalty, she would probably swear a vow of silence.

"Cop a feel in a dark hallway? A little slap and tickle in a broom closet?" she asked.

"I'm too old to cop a feel. And I don't 'slap and tickle' either, whatever that is. I fuck."

Her head jerked back at his blunt statement, her eyes widening behind the dark frames. Even with the din of chatter and laughter flowing around them, he caught her sharp gasp.

A voice sounding suspiciously like that of Gray Chandler, his business partner and best friend—his only friend—hissed a curse at him. How many times had Gray warned him to temper his brusque, straightforward manner? Well, to be more accurate, his friend described Gideon as tactless. Pretty words weren't his forte; honesty was. Normally, he didn't regret his abruptness. Like he'd told her, he didn't indulge in games. But in this moment, he almost regretted it.

Especially if she walked away from him.

"Is that why you stopped me? To proposition me?" She dropped her gaze to the champagne glass in his hand, and with just that glance let him know she didn't buy his pretense of wanting the wine. He shrugged, setting it behind him on one of the high tables scattered around the ballroom.

"Why single me out?" she continued. "Because I'm so beautiful you couldn't help yourself?" she mocked. "Or because I'm a server, and you're a guest in a position of power? What happens if I say no? Will I suddenly find myself relieved of my job?"

Disgust and the first flicker of anger wormed its way through his veins. "Do I want to spend a night with you? Inside you? Yes," he stated, and again her eyes flared wide at his frankness before narrowing. "I told you, I don't lie. I don't play games. But if you decline, then no, you would still have a check and employment at the end of the evening. I don't need to blackmail women into my bed, Camille. Besides, a willing woman, a woman who wants my hands on her body, who pleads for what she knows I can give her, is far more arousing, more pleasurable. And any man worth his dick would value that over a woman who's coerced or forced into handing over something that should be offered or surrendered of her own free will."

She silently studied him, the fire fading from her stare, but something else flicked in those dark eyes. And that "something" had him easing a step closer, yet stopping short of invading her personal space.

"To answer your other question," he murmured. "Why did I single you out? Your first guess was correct. Because you are so beautiful I couldn't help following you around this over-the-top ballroom filled with people who possess more money than sense. The women here can't outshine you. They're like peacocks, spreading their plumage, desperate to be noticed, and here you are among them, like the moon. Bright, alone, above it all and eclipsing every one of them. What I don't understand is how no one else noticed before me. Why every man in this place isn't standing behind me in a line just for the chance to be near you."

Silence swelled around them like a bubble, muting the din of the gala. His words seemed to echo in the cocoon, and he marveled at them. Hadn't he sworn he didn't do pretty words? Yet it had been him talking about peacocks and moons.

What was she doing to him?

Even as the question echoed in his mind, her head tilted back and she stared at him, her lovely eyes darker…hotter. In that moment, he'd stand under a damn balcony and serenade her if she continued looking at him like that. He curled his fingers into his palm, reminding himself with the pain that he couldn't touch her. Still, the only sound that reached his ears was the quick, soft pants breaking on her pretty lips.

As ridiculous as it seemed, he swore each breath slid under his clothes, swept over his skin. He ached to have each moist puff dampen his shoulders, his chest as her fingernails twisted in his hair, dug into his muscles, clinging to him as he drove them both to the point of carnal madness.

The growl prowled up his throat and out of him before he could contain it.

"I—I need to go," she whispered, already shifting back and away from him. "I—" She didn't finish the thought, but turned and waded into the crowd, distancing herself from him.

He didn't follow; she hadn't said no, but she hadn't said yes, either. And though he'd caught the desire in her gaze—his stomach still ached from the gut punch of it—she had to come to him.

Or ask him to come for her.

Rooted where she'd left him, he tracked her movements.

Saw the moment she cleared the mass of people and strode in the direction of the double doors where more tray-bearing staff emerged and exited.

Saw when she paused, palm pressed to one of the panels.

Saw when she glanced over her shoulder in his direction.

Even across the distance of the ballroom, the electric shock of that look whipped through him, sizzled in his veins. Moments later, she disappeared from view. Didn't matter; his feet were already moving in her direction.

That glance, that look. It'd sealed her fate.

Sealed it for both of them.

Two

Shay Camille Neal pushed through the doors leading into the huge, industrial kitchen that wouldn't have been out of place in a Michelin-star restaurant. With a world-famous chef renowned for his temper as well as his magic with food, a sous chef and army of station and line cooks bustling around the stainless steel countertops and range stoves, the area hummed with activity.

Under ordinary circumstances, she would've been enthralled, attempting to soak up whatever knowledge she could from the professionals attending. But the current circumstances were as far from ordinary as chicken nuggets were from coq au vin.

First, as a member of one of the oldest, wealthiest and most influential families in Chicago, she usually attended the Du Sable City Gala as a guest, not a server.

But when her best friend, Bridgette, called her earlier in the afternoon sounding like a foghorn had replaced her voice box, Shay had agreed to take Bridgette's place as a member of the catering staff. Though her friend owned and ran a fledgling food truck business, she still helped mitigate expenses and pay her personal bills with jobs on the side. The position with this particular catering company was one of her regulars, and Bridgette couldn't afford to lose the gig.

Shay had planned on skipping the gala, anyway. Facing a night at home with another binge of *House of Cards* on Netflix versus actually working in the periphery of a famous chef, the choice had been a no-brainer. Besides, Bridgette had assured Shay that most of her duties as an assistant to the line cooks would keep her in the kitchen.

Still, she'd donned a wig, dark brown contacts and glasses, as well as Bridgette's uniform. Because while she'd decided to skip out on the social event of the season, her older brother, Trevor, and his fiancée, Madison Reus—Senator Julian Reus's only daughter—were attending. Trevor already didn't approve of Shay's friendship with Bridgette. If he caught Shay doing anything less-than-becoming of the Neal name, especially because of her best friend, he would lose it. And Shay was pretty certain he would consider prepping vegetables and serving champagne cardinal sins.

In her defense, though, when the catering supervisor shoved a tray of sparkly wine at her and ordered her to make the rounds of the ballroom, she couldn't exactly say no.

Still, everything should've been fine—would've been fine—if not for one Gideon Knight.

Smoky desire coiled in her belly. She set the almost empty tray on one of the stations and pressed a fist to her navel. Not that the futile gesture extinguished the glowing embers.

Swallowing a groan, she strode toward the back of the kitchen and the employee break room. Shutting the door behind her, she entered the bathroom and twisted the faucets, thrusting her palms under the gushing water. Her quick version of a cold shower. Shaking her head at her foolishness, she finished washing her hands, but afterward, instead of returning to the kitchen, she stood in front of the mirror, staring at her reflection. But it wasn't her image she saw.

It was Gideon Knight.

They're like peacocks, spreading their plumage, desperate to be noticed, and here you are among them, like the moon. Bright, alone, above it all and eclipsing every one of them.

She exhaled slowly, the words spoken in that all-things-secret-and-sinful voice echoing in her head. In her chest. And lower. With any other man, she would've waved off the compliment as insincere flattery that tended to roll off men's tongues when they came across the heiress to one of the largest financial management conglomerates in the country. The compliments meant nothing, like dandelion fluff on a breeze. No substance and changing with the wind.

But not with Gideon Knight.

There had been a ring of truth in the blunt observation. As if his description of her wasn't an opinion but fact. She'd just met him, but she couldn't shake the sense that he didn't dole out flowery compliments often. As he'd stated so flatly, he didn't play games.

She believed him. But it only deepened her confusion over why he'd approached her of all people. To most of the attendees in the ballroom, she'd been invisible, inconsequential. Just another staff member there to serve them.

But not to him.

Even in a room full of Chicago's wealthiest and most glamorous people, he stood out. In the way a sleek, silent shark would stand out in a pool of clown fish.

God, she was officially losing it. And she laid the blame squarely at the feet of Gideon Knight.

Because, really, how could any woman stare into those midnight eyes and not forget everything but how she could willingly drown in them, even as he submerged her in a pleasure as dark and stunning as his gaze?

As soon as the illicit thought entered her head an image of him crouched over her, all that midnight-black hair loose from its knot and flowing over his shoulders, tumbling around them, flashed through her mind. Her heart thumped against her chest, and she exhaled an unsteady breath, that flame of unwanted desire dancing low in her belly again. With a mental shove, she thrust the hot image out of her mind, but the vision of how he'd looked just moments ago, when she turned for one last glance, refused to be evicted as easily.

His tailor, whoever he or she was, must've been in love with Gideon because his tuxedo traced his powerful but lean frame. From the wide shoulders and chest that tapered to a slim waist and down to long, muscular legs, he was the picture of urbane elegance and wealth. Strength. Beauty.

Imperial.

The word leaped into her head, and though she wanted to scoff at the description, she couldn't. It fit. With the beautiful eyes, the sharp slant of cheekbones, the arrogant nose, the wide, sensual, almost cruel curve of his mouth and the rock-hard jut of his jaw, he reminded her of a long-ago king from a mysterious Asian country, standing on a wall, an unseen wind teasing his long black hair as he surveyed the land he ruled. Hard, shrewd, somehow removed from the masses.

He would've been completely intimidating if not for the incongruity of all that hair pulled into a knot at the back of his head. Someone so polished, so sophisticated, so rigid in his appearance wearing a…man bun.

It was the rebellious flouting of the unspoken, constricting rules that governed their social realm that had stirred a curiosity she couldn't erase. Even now.

You're being ridiculous.

Shaking her head, she emitted a sound of self-directed disgust and yanked a brown paper towel from the dispensary. She quickly dried her hands, tossed the now damp towel in the trash and strode from the bathroom. With at least another three hours of work ahead of her, she couldn't afford to remain hiding back here any longer. More prep work awaited her, as dinner hadn't even been served yet—

The door to the break room swung open, and she barely managed to stifle her startled gasp.

The tall, imposing figure of Gideon Knight filled the doorway.

Her heart lodged in her throat. What the hell was he doing back here? But only seconds passed before the answer whispered through her skull.

You.

Denial, swift and firm, rose within her. But it couldn't extinguish the kindling of desire and traitorous, *foolish* hope.

"What are you doing here?" she demanded, swiping her already-dry palms down the sides of her pants. And when his gaze took in the nervous gesture, she cursed herself for betraying her agitation to this man.

"Looking for you."

Excitement fluttered in her before she could smother the reaction. Crossing her arms over her chest, she frowned. Fought the instinctive urge to retreat from the intense, sexual magnetism that seemed to pour off him and vibrate in the room.

"Well, I need to return to work." She pretended to glance down at the slim, gold-faced watch on her wrist. "So, if you'll excuse me…"

An emotion crossed his face, but was there and gone before she could decipher it. Probably irritation at being told no. "I wanted to apol—"

But the rest of his explanation snapped off as the room plummeted into darkness.

Three

A cry slipped out of Shay, panic clawing at her throat.

The deep, thick dark pressed down on her chest like a weight, cutting off her breath.

What was going on? What happened? Why…?

"Camille." The sound of that calm voice carrying an undercurrent of steel snapped her out of the dizzying fall into hysteria. Hands wrapped around both her upper arms, the grip firm, steadying. His voice and his touch grounded her, although her pulse continued to thud and echo in her head like a hammer. "Easy." One of his hands slid up her arm, over her shoulder and slipped around the back of her neck. Squeezed. "Stay with me. Breathe."

She closed her eyes, as if that could block out the utter lack of light. Still, she latched on to him—his voice, his fresh yet earthy scent of wind and sandal-wood, the solid density of the forearms she'd at some point clutched. Seconds, minutes—hell, it felt like hours—passed while she focused on calming her racing heart, on breathing. And soon, the sense of being buried alive started to lift.

His hold on her arm and neck never eased.

As the initial bite of panic slowly unhinged its jaws, the weight of his touch—the security and comforting effect of it—penetrated her fear.

"—I'm sorry." Embarrassed, she heard a wobbly chuckle escape her. Belatedly, she loosened her grip on him and dropped her arms. "God, I don't... I'm not even afraid of the dark," she whispered.

"You have nothing to apologize for," he reassured her.

His hands abandoned her neck and arm, but one located and clasped her fingers. In the next instant, a pale blue glow appeared. A cell phone. The illumination barely pushed back the inky thickness surrounding them, but it highlighted his face, and relief weakened her knees. Only moments ago, she'd wanted to get as far away from him as possible. And now her eyes stung with gratefulness for his serene presence. For not being alone.

"I need to go see if I can find out what's going on. Here." Holding the cell out in front of him, he carefully guided her to the couch against the far wall. Still holding her hand, he lowered her to the cushion. "Will you be all right? I have to take my cell with me to try and either get a call or text out. I promise to return in a few minutes."

"Of course." She nodded, injecting a vein of steel into her voice. God, she was stronger than this. "I'll be fine here."

In the cell's minimal light, she caught his steady, measuring stare. "Good," he said after a few moments, returning her nod. "I'll be right back."

He disappeared, returning her to the dark. She focused on maintaining even breathing, reminding herself she hadn't been catapulted into a deep pit where terrifying, malformed things lurked, eager for the chance to take a bite out of her. She really shouldn't have watched Stephen King's *It* last night…

"Camille."

She jerked her head up, and once more that rush of relief washed over her as Gideon and his beautiful light appeared in front of her again.

"Hey," she said, unable to prevent the emotion from flooding her voice. "Were you able to find out anything?" Please let it be something fixable and short-lived, like the owner of this mansion had forgotten to pay his power bill.

"Blackout," he explained, tone grim, and her heart plummeted toward her stomach. "I wasn't able to get a call out, but I was able to send and receive a couple of texts to a contact on the police force. It's city-wide. They're advising people to remain where they are, which," he continued, his full lips flattening for a brief second, "won't be an issue with us. I overheard security speaking to the chef and his staff. The tech guru who owns this overcompensating monstrosity of a home installed a so-called cutting-edge security system. And with the blackout, it's malfunctioned. We're all locked in for the foreseeable future."

She expelled a pent-up breath, pinching the bridge of her nose. Where was Trevor? Were he and Madison okay? What about Bridgette? Sick and in the dark? More than ever, Shay cursed leaving her phone in her car. Bridgette had warned her that her supervisor frowned on the staff having cells on them, so she'd stashed hers in her glove compartment, but now…

"We're going to be fine, Camille," Gideon said, his rough silk voice dragging her away from her worried thoughts. "Most likely, the blackout will only last several hours, and hopefully the boy genius will have his system worked out by them," he finished drily.

In spite of the anxiety over her brother and friend that still inundated her, she snorted. "Boy genius?"

Gideon arched a black eyebrow. "Have you seen him? He can't be more than twenty-three. I swear, I can still smell the milk on his breath."

This time she snickered, belatedly palming her mouth to contain her amusement. "So you're what? The ripe old age of thirty? Thirty-three? And if you're here as a guest, then that means you must be at least wealthy or connected enough to have been invited. Which makes you what, Mr. Knight?" she asked, narrowing her eyes. "An idle man living off his family name and money? Or a successful businessman in his own right?"

She didn't know him, but he struck her as the latter.

There was nothing about him that screamed idle. No, the sharklike intelligence that gleamed from his dark eyes belonged to a man who forged his own path, not one satisfied with walking the one others had paved for him.

He didn't immediately reply, but treated her to another of his intense gazes. He seemed to peer beneath skin and bone to the soul. To her secrets. With effort, she didn't shirk away from his scrutiny, instead notching her chin up and meeting his eyes without flinching.

Something glinted in his gaze, and the faint light from his phone tricked her into believing it might be admiration.

"I own and run a start-up that provides privately held companies with their equity needs. I suppose you can say we've been successful."

The vague and carefully constructed answer didn't stop recognition from rocking her. Start-up? As in KayCee Corp start-up? He couldn't possibly be *the* Gideon Knight, founder of the corporation that had taken the financial world by storm five years ago? If so, he was either exceedingly modest or being cagey with information.

Because KayCee Corp had been more than "successful." The electronic platform serviced major businesses, helping them track their shares with its top-of-the-line, unrivaled software. They'd recently announced their intentions to branch out and work with companies that were rolling out their initial public offerings. Though Trevor tried to keep Shay securely ensconced in the Social Development branch of

RemingtonNeal Inc., their family business, she knew of KayCee Corp. Knew that Trevor desperately longed to acquire it.

Her wig, contacts and glasses concealed her true identity, but she still lifted her fingers to her cheek as if Gideon could see beneath the camouflage. Her throat tightened. Now would be a good time to come clean about who he sat with in the dark. But something held her back. Something, hell... She could identify it even without him searching her soul.

In that ballroom, Gideon Knight had gazed upon her with fascination, admiration...hunger. And he'd had no idea she was Shay Neal, heiress to a global financial empire. Not that she was an ugly duckling in a lake full of swans, but she bore no illusions. Her money, social status and connections were often just as much, if not more, of an allure than her appearance.

But not for him.

Even now, his dark stare roamed her face, lingering on her eyes before drifting over her cheekbones, her jaw, her mouth. Though it belied reason, she swore she could feel his gaze stroke over her skin. An illicit, mysterious, desire-stoking caress.

And here, in the isolated depths of this mansion, she wanted more.

Even if just for a little while.

The cloak of anonymity bestowed her with a gift of boldness—of freedom—she didn't ordinarily possess.

"I wonder what's going through your head right now?" he murmured, drawing her from her thoughts. "And would you honestly tell me?"

That would be a no. "Careful, Mr. Knight," she drawled, tone dry. "You're beginning to sound a little too Edward Cullen-ish for my comfort."

"Last time I checked, I didn't sparkle in the sunlight or age out at eighteen years old. Although I do admit to a little biting. And liking it."

A blast of heat barreled through her, warring with surprise over his recognition of her *Twilight* reference. Curling her fingers into her palms, she willed the searing desire to abate, but it continued to burn a path along her veins.

"Still blunt, I see," she said, and no way could he miss the hoarseness rasping her voice. "You weren't lying when you claimed not to play games."

"Am I making you uncomfortable, Camille?" he asked, his head cocking to the side. His eyes narrowed on her, as if searching out the answer for himself.

She should say yes. Should order him to keep his straight-no-chaser compliments and need-stirring comments to himself.

Instead, she matched his head tilt. "And if I said you were?"

"Then I'd go out there in that kitchen and drag one of those chefs in here so you wouldn't be. Is that what you want?"

She shook her head, the denial almost immediate. "No," she said, although wisdom argued she should have him invite the whole crew into this small room. Protect her from herself. The self that couldn't help wondering if those stark angles softened with pleasure. Wondering if that hard-looking mouth became more pliable.

Wondering if that icy shield of control shattered under desire's flame?

A shiver danced over her skin. Waltzed along her nerve endings.

She was the moth dancing too close to those flames.

"What do you want?" he pressed, the deep timbre of his voice dipping lower.

He didn't move, didn't inch closer to her on the couch. But God, all that intensity crowded her, rubbed over her, slipped inside her. He wasn't a coy or playful man; he grasped the wealth of possibilities that question carried. And he offered her the choice of not addressing them...or taking all of them.

A lifetime of playing by the rules slowly unraveled beneath his heated stare. His question vibrated between them, a gauntlet thrown down. A red flag waved.

"Too many things to possibly number in the space of a blackout," she finally replied. Truth. And evasion. "But I'm fine with you here with me." She paused, and with her heart tapping an unsteady rhythm against her chest, added, "Only you."

A fierce approval and satisfaction flashed like diamonds in his eyes. "Good," he said, those same emotions reflected in the one word. "Because now we don't have to share this with anyone else." Reaching down, he picked up a plate and set it on the cushion between them. A grin curved her lips at the sight of the braised lamb, roasted vegetable medley and risotto piled on the fine china.

"Now, that's lovely," he murmured, his gaze not on the dinner but on her face.

She ducked her head, wishing the strands of the wig weren't tied back in a bun so they could hide the red stain creeping up her neck and flooding her face.

"You're certainly resourceful," she said, reaching for an asparagus tip. "Or sneaky."

His soft snort echoed between them. "I've been accused of both before. And both are just words. Whatever works to achieve my goal."

"Yes, I clearly remember your goal for this evening. You didn't mince words out there earlier. I guess you've achieved your aim. Spending the night with me."

Why had she brought up that conversation? What had possessed her to remind him of his claim to be with her—*inside* her? To see that glint of hunger again? To tempt him? God, she was flirting with danger. And doing so with a rashness that bordered on recklessness.

"Do you really want to dive into that discussion right now, Camille?" The question—a tease, a taunt—set her pulse off on a rapid tattoo.

Yes.

No.

"Not on an empty stomach," she whispered, retreating. From the faint quirk of his lips—the first hint of a smile she'd glimpsed on his austere face—he caught her withdrawal. "And you wouldn't happen to be hiding a bottle of wine over there, would you?"

The quirk deepened, and her heart stuttered. Actually skipped a couple beats at the beauty of that half smile. Jesus, he would be absolutely devastating if he ever truly let go. Her fingertips itched with the urge to trace those sensual lips. To curb the need, she brought her hands to her pants, intent on rubbing them down her thighs. But stopped herself, recalling they were damp from the food she'd just eaten.

"Take this." He reached inside his jacket and offered her a small white handkerchief.

Startled, she accepted it, again struck with how perceptive he seemed to be.

"Thank you," she murmured.

For the next half hour, they dined on the pilfered food, and as stellar and flavorful as the cuisine was, it didn't steal her attention like the man across from her. He...fascinated her. And after they finished, when he asked her if she would be fine with him turning off the phone's light to conserve the battery, she okayed it without hesitation.

Though he was basically a stranger to her, he emanated safety. Comfort. As if he would release all that barely leashed mercilessness on her behalf instead of against her. Maybe that made her fanciful, too. But in the dark, she could afford it.

Perhaps the blackness affected him in a similar fashion, because he opened up to her—well, as much as someone as controlled as Gideon Knight probably did. They spoke of mundane things. Hobbies. Worst dates. The best way to spend a perfect, lazy afternoon. All so simple, but she hung on every word. Enjoyed it. Enjoyed him.

Enjoyed the lack of sight that peeled away barriers.

Reveled in the desire that thrummed just below the surface like a drum keeping time, marching them forward to…what? She didn't know. And for the first time in longer than she could remember, she didn't weigh the effect of every word, the consequence of every action on the Neal family name.

Here, with him, she was just…Camille.

"We'll never see each other again once the lights come back on," she said. And it was true. They'd never see each other as Camille and Gideon, even if they happened to cross paths in the future. Because then, she would once more be Shay Neal of the Chicago Neals. "That almost makes me…sad," she confessed, then scoffed, shaking her head, though he couldn't see the gesture. "Ridiculous, right?"

"Why?" he asked. "Honesty is never silly. It's too rare to be ridiculous."

A twinge of guilt pinged inside her chest. She was being dishonest about the most basic thing—her identity. "Because fantasies are for teenage girls, not for grown women who know better."

"And what do you believe you know, Camille?"

She turned toward him, toward the temptation of his voice. "That if not for a citywide blackout, a man like you wouldn't be with me…" She paused. "Talking."

"I don't know if I should be more offended that you're belittling me or yourself with that statement." A whisper of sound and then fingers—questing, gentle, but so damn sure—stroked across her jaw, her temple, the strangely callused tips abrading her skin. What did a man like him do to earn that hardened skin that spoke of hard labor, not crunching numbers? "Yes, I do. It annoys me more that you would demean yourself. A woman like you," he murmured. "Beautiful. Intelligent. Bold. Confident. What man wouldn't want to spend time with you? Only one too blind or stupid to see who stands right before his eyes. Read any financial blog or journal, Camille. I'm not a stupid man."

She snorted, trying to mask the flame licking at her from the inside out. Cover the yearning his words caused deep within her. "How did you manage to compliment yourself and reprimand me at the same time?"

But he ignored her attempt to inject levity into the thick, pulsing atmosphere. No, instead, he swept another caress over her skin. This time, brushing a barely there touch to the curve of her bottom lip. She trembled. And God, he had to sense it, to feel it. Because he repeated it.

"I don't date," he informed her, and the frankness of the statement caught her off guard. Almost made her forget the long fingers still cradling her jaw.

Almost.

"Excuse me?" she breathed.

"I don't date," he repeated. "I know something, too, Camille. Relationships, commitments—they're lies we tell ourselves so we can justify using each other. Sex. Need. Passion—they're honest. The body can't lie. Lust is the great equalizer regardless of social status, race or tax bracket. So no, I rescind my earlier statement. If not for this blackout, it's very possible we wouldn't have passed these last couple of hours talking. But I don't care if we were in a ballroom or a boardroom, I would've noticed you. I would've wanted you. I would've done everything in my power to convince you to trust me with your body, your pleasure."

Oh damn.

She couldn't breathe. Couldn't move. Suspended by the hunger swamping her.

"Your turn, moonbeam," he said, his hand falling away from her face. And she immediately missed his touch, that firm grasp. Because he couldn't see her, she lifted her fingers to the skin that continued to tingle. "Tell me again what you know."

Moonbeam. The endearment reminded her of their conversation in the ballroom. Her brain argued that the word had nothing to do with love or sweetness and everything to do with hunger and darkness, and yet she jolted at the coiling in her lower belly.

"I know you're telling me you haven't changed your mind about wanting to spend the night with me. Inside me," she added, on a soft, almost hushed rush of breath.

"And have you changed yours?"

From the moment you called me your moon.

The truth reverberated against her skull, but she clenched her jaw, preventing it from escaping. Her defenses had started crumbling long before he'd come looking for her.

Did this make her a cliché? He wasn't the first

man to profess he wanted her, but he was the first she longed to touch with a need that unnerved her. She'd never yearned for a man's hands on her body as much as she longed for Gideon Knight's big, elegant, long-fingered ones stroking over her breasts. Or gripping her hips, holding her steady for a deep, hot possession that had her sex spasming in anticipation...in preparation.

She exhaled a breath. Right, he still waited for her answer, and she suspected he wouldn't make a move, wouldn't feather another of those caresses over her until she gave it to him.

"Yes," she confessed, her heart thudding heavily against her rib cage.

"About what, Camille?" he pressed, relentless. "What have you decided? What do you want?"

He wasn't granting her a reprieve; he was making her say it. Making her lay herself bare.

Her sense of self-preservation launched a last-ditch effort to save her from who she'd become in the dark. Who she'd become in that ballroom. But desire crushed it, and she willingly surrendered to the irresistible lure of freedom...of him.

"You," she whispered. "I've decided on you."

She slid across the small space separating them and located his face. A soft groan rolled up her throat, and she didn't even try and trap it. Not when she curved her hand around the strong jut of his jaw, the faintest bristles of what would become a five o'clock shadow abrading her palm. Unable to stop, she stroked the pad of her thumb over the mouth she had been craving since she first noticed him.

Strong teeth sank into the flesh of her thumb, not hurting her but exerting enough pressure that she gasped. Then whimpered.

How had she gone twenty-five years without being aware that spot connected to her sex? That it would make her thighs clench on an ache so sweet, it maddened her?

Another gasp broke free of her, this one of surprise, as his fingers closed around her arms and abruptly dragged her to her feet. She swayed, but he didn't release her until she steadied. Then the sudden flare of light from his cell phone startled her again. After the dark, the pale glow seemed almost too bright. She blinked, glancing from the screen to the shadows it cast over Gideon's face.

"Why…" She waved toward the phone. "What about saving the battery?"

He shook his head, his features sharper, appearing to be hewn from flint. Except for those glittering, almost fevered eyes. *Oh wow…* Such intensity and…and greed there. It stirred her own hunger, stoking the fire inside her until she burned with it.

"I don't give a damn. I need to see you," he growled, shrugging out of his jacket and tossing it to the floor. Still controlled, but the movement carried an edge. And it thrilled her. "Take off your shirt, Camille. Show me what you've decided I can have."

With trembling fingers, she reached for the buttons of her white shirt. It required several attempts, but she managed to open it, and with his black gaze fixed on her, slipped it off. Warm air kissed her bared shoulders, the tops of her breasts and stomach.

A part of her argued that she should feel at least a modicum of modesty, and maybe Shay would. But not Camille.

As crazy as it seemed, here, with Gideon, she had become a different person. The flip side of the same coin. Normally reserved, bound by expectations and family. But now... uninhibited, free to indulge in her own selfish desires.

"Gorgeous," he rasped. "So fucking gorgeous. Come here." He beckoned.

His almost growled compliment stole more of her breath.

"Your turn," she ordered, remaining in place, although her fingers already prickled to stroke the skin and muscle hidden beneath the thin veneer of civility presented by his tuxedo. "Show me what you promised me I can take."

His fingers tightened around the edges of his shirt, and for a moment, she feared—hoped—he would just rip it off. But once more, that control reemerged, and he removed his cuff links, tossing them carelessly on top of his jacket. Then, button by button, he revealed himself to her.

She stared at the male animal before her. Miles and miles of smooth flesh stretched taut over tight muscle and tendon. Wide shoulders, a deep chest. Narrowed waist. A corrugated ladder of abs. A thin, silky line of hair started just above a shadowed navel and traveled below, disappearing into the waistband of his suit pants. And darker swirls and shapes she couldn't make out spread over the left side of his ribs, emphasizing the hint of wildness, of fierceness he couldn't quite conceal.

Perfection.

He was utter perfection.

This time, he didn't need to demand she come to him. Shay covered the distance on her own, arms already extended. With a hum of pleasure, she settled her palms on him, smoothed them up to his shoulders, pushing the shirt down his arms. Then she returned to her exploration. Scraping her nails over small, flat nipples, mapping the thin network of veins under his skin, following the path of hair that started midchest. Dragging her fingertips down the delineated ridge of muscles covering his stomach. Tracing the black lines of his tattoo, wishing she could aim more light on it so she could decipher its shape.

He stood still, letting her tour him without interference, though he fairly hummed with intensity, with barely leashed power.

"Are you finished yet?" he growled, and she tilted her head back to meet his hooded gaze, her fingers settling on the band of his pants.

"Not even close," she breathed. "Kiss me."

Someone with his extraordinary sense of restraint most likely didn't take or obey orders from anyone. But with a flash in those eyes, he gripped the bun at the back of her head and tugged. She gave only a brief thought to the security of the wig before her neck arched. The next breath she took was his.

Her groan was ragged and so needy it should've embarrassed her. Maybe it would tomorrow in the harsh light of day. But tonight, with his tongue twisting and tangling with hers, she couldn't care. Not when he tasted like everything delicious but forbidden—chocolate-flavored wine, New York cheesecake, impropriety and wickedness. Not when he nipped at her bottom lip, then sucked it, soothing and enhancing the sting before returning to devour her mouth. As if she, too, was something he knew he shouldn't have but couldn't resist.

He lifted his head, taking that lovely mouth with him, and she cried out in disappointment. But he shushed her with hard, stinging kisses to the corner of her lips, along the line of her jaw, down her chin and neck…over the tops of her breasts. In seconds, he stripped her of her bra, baring her to him. His big hands lifted, cupping her, molding her to him. To his pleasure. And hers.

She grasped his shoulders, clung to him, her ability to think, to move, to breathe a thing of the past as he lowered his head to her flesh. All she could do was stand there with increasingly wobbly knees and receive each lick, suckle and draw of those sensual lips and tongue. And enjoy them.

Unable not to touch the lure of his hair, she swept her fingers over his head, tunneling them under the knot containing the midnight strands. Eager to see him undone, she briefly wrestled with the thick locks, freeing the tie restraining them. The rough silk fell over her wrists, cool and dense, sliding through her fingers.

"Oh," she whispered, at a loss for words as the strands tumbled around his sharp cheekbones and strong jaw. They should've softened his features—should have. Instead, they only emphasized the stark planes of his face and his visceral sexuality.

"God, you're beautiful." The praise exited her mouth without her permission, but she couldn't regret the words. Not when they were the truth.

Pulling his mouth away from her breasts, he dragged a hot, wet path up her chest, her throat, until he recaptured her mouth. This kiss was hotter, wilder, as if the tether on his control had frayed, and suddenly, her one purpose was to see it snap completely.

With a small whimper, she trailed her hand over his shoulder, chest and torso, not stopping until she cupped his rigid length through his pants.

Damn. She shivered, both need and feminine anxiety tumbling in her belly and lower. He more than filled her palm. Reflexively, she squeezed his erection. God, he was so thick, hard...big.

A rumble emanated from his chest, and his larger hand covered hers, pressing her closer, clasping him tighter. His hips bucked against her palm in demand, and she gladly obeyed. Even as his mouth ravaged hers, she stroked him, loving the growl that rolled out of him. Wanting more.

Impatient, Shay attacked the clasp of his pants, jerking them open and tugging down the zipper in a haste that would later strike her as unseemly. But right now, she didn't give a damn. Nothing mattered but his bare, pulsing flesh in her hand. Touching him.

But just as she reached for him, an implacable grip circled her wrist, stilling her frantic movements.

"Not yet, moonbeam." He lifted one of her arms and placed an openmouthed kiss to the center of her palm, the resulting feeling radiating straight to her damp, quivering sex. With a quick crush of his lips to hers, he swiftly divested her of her remaining clothes and shoes, leaving her trembling and naked before him, except for the decidedly *un*sexy plain, black panties.

A burst of self-consciousness flared inside her chest, and she fought not to edge backward, away from the weak glow of the cell phone's light. But as if he'd read her intentions, Gideon cupped her hip, preempting any movement she might've made to hide.

"When a man stands before beauty like yours, there's only one position he's supposed to be in," he murmured. Slowly, he lowered himself to his knees, tipping his head back to continue to meet her gaze. "You deserve to be worshipped." He swept his lips across her stomach. "And pleasured." Another sweep, but over the top of her sex. Heat coiled tight, and her core clenched at the tantalizing caress. "Give me permission to give you that."

It might've emerged as an order, but he wouldn't continue without her go-ahead. She somehow knew that.

"Yes," she breathed, tunneling her fingers through his hair. Holding on tight.

With a deliberate pace that had her internally

screaming, he drew her underwear down her legs and helped her step free of them. Big, elegant hands brushed up her calves and thighs, and once more she wondered at the calluses adding a hint of roughness to the caress. But then she ceased thinking at all.

"Gideon," she cried out, fisting his hair, trying to pull him away or tug him closer—she didn't know. Couldn't decide. Not when pleasure unlike anything she'd ever experienced struck her with great bolts of lightning. Jesus, his lips, his tongue… They were voracious. Feasting on her, leaving no part of her unexplored, untouched. Long, luxurious swirls, decadent and wicked laps and sucks… He drove her insane with pleasure.

Just as he'd promised. Just as he'd assured her she deserved.

He spread her wider, hooking her leg over one of his wide shoulders, granting himself easier access. Like a ravenous beast, he growled against her sensitive, wet sex, and the vibration shoved her closer to the edge of release.

"You're so fucking sweet," he rasped, nuzzling her. "So fucking sweet and pure. A man could get addicted to you. But you have more to give me, don't you, baby? I'm a greedy bastard, and I want it all." He uttered the last words almost as if to himself, and with one palm molded to her behind, he dragged the other up the inside of her spread thighs.

Then he was filling her. Two fingers plunged inside her, and like a match struck to dry kindling, she sparked, flared, exploded into flames. Dimly, she caught his rough encouragement of "That's it, baby. That's it." She loosened a hand from his hair and clapped it over her lips, muffling her cries as she came against his mouth, her hips rolling and jerking.

Raw, dirty ecstasy, stripped to its barest essentials. That's who she'd become in this moment as he lapped up every evidence of her desire from her flesh, from the insides of her thighs.

"Please," she begged, weakly pushing his head away as he circled her with tender but relentless strokes. "I can't."

"That's nothing but a challenge to me, moonbeam," he rumbled, standing, his mouth damp. But when he lowered his head and took her lips in a torrid kiss that replicated how he'd just consumed her, she didn't back away from the flavor of herself on his lips and tongue. No, she opened wider to him, turned on so bright it ached.

Palming the back of her thighs, he hiked her in the air. On reflex she wound her legs around his waist. He crossed to the couch, and with each bump of her swollen, sensitive core against his stomach, that recently satiated heat flickered back to life, and she moaned with each caress.

Her back met the cushions, and Gideon towered over her, half his face cast in shadow. That obsidian gaze never left hers as he removed a thin wallet from his pants pocket and withdrew a condom. He tossed it down, next to her feet, and then she watched, enraptured, as he stripped off his clothes. Her breath snagged in her throat. *Jesus*. He'd been stunning in a perfectly tailored tuxedo. But naked, the trappings torn away, all that thick, midnight hair falling around his face and broad shoulders... He was *magnificent*. Long legs, powerful thighs... Good God, she'd felt him, but *seeing* him... Like the rest of him, his erection was proud, beautiful. Perfect.

As if of their own volition, her arms lifted, beckoning him to her. He tore open the foil square and sheathed himself then came to her, moving the cell phone to the floor next to them. His hard body covered hers, and a sigh escaped her at the contact. For a second, she couldn't smother the sense of never having felt so cherished, so protected.

"Ready, moonbeam?" he murmured, raising off her slightly. Grasping her hand in his, he brought it between their bodies. As he'd done earlier, he wrapped her fingers around his thick length. "Show me," he ordered, planting his palms on either side of her head, granting her control.

Even if she harbored the smallest seed of doubt about this illicit encounter in the dark—which she didn't—his gesture would've eradicated it. Her chest tightened, her heart thudding against her rib cage. But her hand was steady as she guided him to her entrance. Shifting her palm to his taut behind, she pushed as she lifted her hips, taking him inside. Fully. Widening her thighs, she didn't stop until he was buried within her.

She gasped, a ripple rocking her body. God, he was *everywhere*. Over her, around her, inside her. So deep inside her. The weight and length of him stretched her, burned her, and she flexed against him, her flesh struggling to accommodate the sweet invasion.

His eyes closed, and he bowed his head, pressing his forehead to hers, his breath pulsing over her lips. Tension vibrated through him, strained the muscles in his arms, stilled his large frame. Long moments later, he lifted his head, and the effort to hold back was etched onto his features.

"Gideon," she whispered, waiting until he lifted his ridiculously dense lashes to meet her eyes. "Let go."

As if those two words sliced through the last threads of his restraint, he groaned and lost it.

On the tail of another of those sexy snarls, he dragged his erection free, lighting up nerve endings like an airport runway, before snapping his hips and thrusting back inside her. Driving her breath from her lungs and a wail of pleasure from her throat.

Oh God. She wasn't going to survive this.

Pleasure inundated her as he plunged into her body. Over and over, relentlessly. He hooked an arm under her leg, tugging it higher and impossibly wider. With a choked cry, she wrapped her arms around his neck, holding on, a willing sacrifice to his possession. He rode her, wild and untethered, giving her no quarter. Not that she asked for any. She loved it. Every roll of his hips, every slap of flesh against flesh, every rake of his teeth over her shoulder.

In his arms, under his body, she transformed into a sexual creature who lived, breathed for him, for the ecstasy only he could give.

Electric pulses crackled down her back, sizzling

at the base of her spine. Every thrust intensified the sensation. When he slid a hand between them and rubbed her, an avalanche of pleasure rushed toward her, burying her, stealing her consciousness. But not before Gideon stiffened above her, his deep, tortured groan echoing in her ear, rumbling against her chest.

"Camille," he whispered, and it sounded like a benediction, a prayer.

And as she tightened her arms around him before sinking under, she foolishly wished to be his answer.

Four

Gideon frowned, reaching out to shut off his alarm. Drowsiness still clung to him, a warm lassitude weighing down his muscles, and he wanted to savor it instead of drive it away. But that damn alarm.

"Damn it," he grumbled, but instead of hitting the digital clock on his bedside table, he slapped air. No table. No clock. Hell, no bed.

He sat up, groaning at the pull of muscle in his lower back. Tunneling his fingers through his hair, he dragged it back from his face, scanning the small room with a television, a long table against the far wall, a short row of gray metal lockers and the couch he was sprawled on.

The blackout.

Camille.

As if her name released a floodgate, the memories

from the previous night poured forward. Serving Camille dinner. Talking with her. Kissing her. Being inside her. In response, his body stirred, hardening as image after image of her twisting and arching beneath him, taking him, flashed across his mind's screen like an HD movie.

He whipped around, scanning the room with new eyes, searching for any sign of her. But only his clothes and the empty dinner plates littered the floor. No Camille.

Adrenaline streaked through his veins, and he snatched his pants from the floor, dragging them on. She couldn't have gotten far. Weak morning light trickled into the room through the high window, so it still had to be pretty early. And with the house still locked down...

No, not locked down. For the first time, the low drone of the small refrigerator in the far corner reached his ears. Power had returned, which meant the blackout had ended. Still, how much of a head start could she have? He had to find her.

Just as he swept his shirt off the floor a Queen song erupted into the stifling room. It'd been this that he'd initially mistaken for his alarm, but it was his mom's special ringtone. He strode the few steps required to recover the phone from beside the couch, arching his eyebrows in surprise that it still had power.

Only 3 percent, he noted, swiping a thumb across the screen.

"Hey, Mom," he said in greeting, fastening buttons as he spoke. "I have very little battery left, so I can't talk long. But I'm okay—"

"Gideon," she said, and her solemn tone cut him off.

Anxiety and the first spike of fear speared his chest. He'd come to associate that particular note with one thing. And as she murmured, "It's Olivia," his guess proved correct.

Closing his eyes, he straightened his shoulders, bracing himself. "What happened?"

"She's in the hospital. I had to take her in last night." Her sigh echoed in his ear; the weariness and worry tore at him. "Gideon." She paused. "She saw the news about Trevor Neal's engagement."

A familiar anger awakened in his chest, stretching to life.

"I'm on my way."

Gideon exited his sister's private room on the behavioral health floor of Mercy Hospital & Medical Center, quietly shutting the door behind him.

Behavioral health. Fancy words for psychiatric ward.

Scrubbing a hand down his face, he strode through the hall to the waiting area where his mother and her parents perched on chairs. The three of them zeroed in on him as soon as he entered the small space with the connected seating and mounted television. God, it reeked of sadness and exhaustion. The same emotions etched in his mother's and grandparents' faces.

"How is she?" his mom asked, rising.

Frustration, grief and anger choked him, and for a moment he couldn't speak. Instead he gathered his mother in his arms and hugged her close. Ai Knight had been his rock—his family's rock—since his dad died when Gideon was nine years old. Though his grandparents were here now, that hadn't always been the case. When she'd married Gideon's father, they'd disowned her. As immigrants from Kaiping who'd settled in Canada in the 1960s, they'd wanted their only daughter to marry a Chinese man from the "Four Counties," not a Caucasian from Chicago. But Ai had, and after she'd moved to the US with him, she and her parents hadn't spoken for almost ten years. But since then they'd reconciled, and his grandparents had even moved to Chicago to be closer to Ai and their grandchildren. Which Gideon was thankful for, since his father had been a foster child, and so his mother's parents were the only extended family he and his sister had.

"Gideon?" his mother prompted.

Sighing, he released her. God, he hated seeing her here in this room, the gravity of her daughter's illness weighing down her delicate but strong shoulders.

"Sleeping. They have her heavily sedated at the moment," he replied. Which wasn't much of an answer.

"How long will she be here?" his grandmother inquired, stretching her arm out and clasping her daughter's hand.

"I'm not sure, Po Po," he said, using the Taishanese term for maternal grandmother. His grandfather—his gung gung—remained silent, but settled a hand on his wife's thin knee. "The doctor said definitely the next seventy-two hours. Maybe more."

They remained there, silent but connected through physical touch. After several moments, he squeezed his mom's shoulder. "Can I talk to you out in the hall?"

She nodded, following him out of the waiting

room—and out of earshot of his grandparents. They might be a tight family, but there were some things even they didn't know, and Gideon preferred to keep it that way when it came to his younger sister.

"What happened?" he demanded, softening the hard tone of his question by enfolding her hand in his.

"Since the announcement of Trevor's engagement, I've tried my best to keep her protected from the news. Even going on her computer and phone and blocking those society sites. But I knew that was only prolonging the inevitable. And last night, she found out. I heard her sobbing all the way from downstairs, Gideon," she whispered, the dark eyes she'd bequeathed to him liquid with tears. "I ran to her room and found her curled up in a ball on the floor of her bedroom, crying uncontrollably. Unable to stop. I was afraid. So I called the ambulance."

He ground his teeth together, an ache flaring along his jaw as he struggled to imprison the blistering stream of curses that would not only offend his mother but would be pointless.

Nothing he said could ease his sister's anguish. And no amount of release could extinguish his hatred toward Trevor Neal, the bastard responsible for shattering the kind, loving, fragile woman who'd given him her heart. A heart Trevor had trampled, then tossed aside like trash.

It'd been a year ago, but to Olivia, Trevor's betrayal might as well as have been yesterday. She'd kept her love affair with the CEO of RemingtonNeal, Inc. from Gideon, because he and Trevor had no love lost between them; they'd been rivals and enemies for years. Gideon had never hidden his hatred toward the other man.

Which explained why Trevor had targeted her in the first place.

He'd romanced Olivia, manipulated her into falling in love with him, making promises of a future together. Then, out of the blue, he'd cruelly dumped her. But that hadn't been the worst of it. Olivia had been pregnant with his child. Trevor hadn't cared. He'd even ordered her to get an abortion, which she'd refused. But in the end, it hadn't mattered. She'd miscarried, and the loss had sunk her into a depression that had begun to lift only a couple months ago. Seeking to protect her from any further hurt, Gideon and his mother had kept the information about the engagement to themselves.

But now this had happened.

"I'm sorry." His mother interrupted his thoughts by cupping his cheek. "I know this has to be difficult for you, too. This whole engagement thing. How're you doing?"

He covered her hand with his and then pressed a kiss to her palm before lowering it. Schooling his features, he submerged the jagged knife of pain and humiliation beneath a sheet of ice. "I'm fine, Mom. I'm not the one who needs your worry today."

She didn't immediately reply, studying him. "I'm a mother. I have enough concern to spread around evenly," she said, and amusement whispered through him. "She was your fiancée, Gideon," she pointed out, as if he didn't know. "Cheating on you was hurtful enough, but this? And with him of all people?" She shook her head. "There's no way you can possibly be 'fine.'"

"Let it go, Mom," he murmured, sliding his hands into the front pockets of his pants and slightly turning away from her incisive gaze. "I have."

Lies.

He would never forget Madison Reus's betrayal. Or forgive it. Not when the man she'd cheated with had been Trevor.

The other man had made it his mission to bring Gideon down a peg. And this latest stunt—pursuing Madison, fucking her and now marrying her—had been a direct hit. Anger at his enemy and his ex swelled within him. Both were selfish, narcissistic and uncaring of who they destroyed.

Especially Trevor.

Gideon had been unable to protect his sister from him the first time. And now she still suffered from his cruelty. It sickened Gideon that he'd failed her, despite the fact that he hadn't known until it was too late. As her older brother, the man in the family, he should've been there. Should've asked questions. Should've...

Damn it. He ruthlessly scrubbed his hands down his face.

Never again. Trevor Neal wouldn't get away unscathed this time.

He would pay. Pay for them all.

Five

Shay approached the dining room entrance, pausing just outside, preparing herself for the first meal of the day. It was breakfast; it shouldn't be an event worthy of deep-breathing techniques. But depending on her brother's mood, it could go either way—calm and pleasant or tap dancing on her last damn nerve. Sighing, she straightened her shoulders and entered.

"Good morning," she said to Trevor, pulling out her chair to his left. As soon as she lowered herself into it, Jana, their maid, appeared at her elbow and set a plate with steaming hot food in front of her. "Thank you, Jana." She smiled at the other woman.

Trevor glanced up from the tablet next to his plate. "You're running late this morning," he said in lieu of a greeting.

"A little bit of a restless night," she explained.

Several restless nights, actually. But she kept that bit of information to herself, since there was no way she could tell her brother what—or rather *who*—had been interrupting her sleep lately.

"Are you okay?" His eyes, hazel like her own, narrowed on her face. "Feeling well?"

There were moments like this, when concern shone in his gaze, that made it hard to remember the increasingly cold and callous man her brother could be. Right now, he was the caring big brother from her childhood who'd affectionately teased her, who'd spent hours watching TV with her when she'd been sick with the flu and bored. That man had started to make rarer appearances over the last few years—since their father had fallen sick and died.

"I'm fine," she replied, cutting into her vegetable omelet. "What am I running late for?"

"The office. You have a meeting with the representative from the ASPCA. You can't afford to be late for that, not with the fund-raising gala for Grace Sanctuary just a few nights away. I'm counting on you to make this a success for not just RemingtonNeal but for Mom's memory," he reminded her.

No pressure. She swallowed the retort. Barely.

While she firmly believed Trevor had created her position and department specifically for her—vice president of Social Development—she did her best for it. Yes, it was an important job—anything bettering their city and the people living there was worthy—but it wasn't her passion. And it damn sure wasn't what she'd attended college and earned a BBA and MBA to do. She'd wanted to join her brother in running RemingtonNeal, but like their controlling, domineering father, he'd shot down that idea.

Usually, Trevor took no interest in her work unless a photo op happened to be attached to it. But Grace Sanctuary belonged to their mother—it had been her pet project before she died, when Shay was eleven and Trevor sixteen. Their father had continued its legacy until he passed, and now they did. The foundation funded various shelters throughout the city, as well as paid veterinarian, adoption and fostering fees for families taking in the animals. The fund-raising gala was important, as the donations from the attendees encompassed a large portion of the budget.

Still, Shay had headed the committee for the gala the past three years, and the last thing she needed was Trevor breathing down her neck or trying to micromanage.

"Everything is going smoothly, and the benefit will be a success like it always has been," she said.

"I know it will. After all, it's in your hands," Trevor praised softly. "I'm sorry if I'm being overbearing, Shay. And if I haven't said it before, thank you. Believe me, I would be a lot more of a pain in the ass if you weren't in charge. I trust you to make this gala the best yet."

Warmth spread through her chest, and she swallowed past the lump of emotion lodged in her throat. Here was the big brother she knew and loved. The one whose approval she valued because it meant so much to her.

"Thank you," she murmured. Then, clearing her throat, she asked, "How's Madison?"

His fiancée had been joining them for breakfast more often lately. Actually, spending more time at the house, period. As if she were already preparing to be mistress of the home.

"She's fine." He picked up his napkin and dabbed at his mouth. "Just so you're aware, I gave her a key. She's dropping by later with an interior designer. There're some things she wants to change in the living and dining rooms, as I do most of my entertaining in those two places. And since she'll soon be living here..." He shrugged. "I didn't think you'd mind, so I told her to go forward with it."

Irritation twinged inside Shay's chest. As usual, Trevor didn't consult her about anything, even when it had to do with her home. Yes, Madison would soon be moving in as his wife, but it'd been Shay's home for twenty-five years. Yet it hadn't occurred to him to ask her opinion, which didn't count for much with her older brother. Again, like their father.

The irony of it always struck her. Trevor and their father had had a...complicated relationship. He'd loved and revered Daniel Shay, constantly seeking his stingy approval, while at the same time, resenting his my-way-and-there's-no-such-thing-as-a-highway attitude when it came to running his company and his family. Especially when it came to raising his only son, who would one day inherit his financial kingdom. Yet, over the years, Trevor had become the reflection of their father. And the battle inside her—the warring factions of anger at his overbearing arrogance and protectiveness for the brother she loved—continued to wage.

But, as she was discovering, it was pointless to argue with Trevor regarding anything having to do with Madison Reus. Winning the hand of a senator's daughter had been a coup for him, and he spoiled her like a princess. And like royalty, Madison accepted it as her due.

That sounded catty even in her own head. *God.* Shay winced, sipping the coffee Jana had set before her.

Doesn't make it any less true, her inner bitch whispered.

"Of course not," she said evenly.

"Good." He nodded. "What're your plans for lunch? We could meet so you can give me an update on the benefit."

She shook her head. "I can't. I'm meeting Bridgette."

Trevor's mouth thinned into a flat, grim line.

Yes, she already got that he didn't like her friendship with the other woman. Bridgette's mother had worked for the Neal family when they were younger. Lonely, Shay had immediately bonded with the precocious, funny little girl who'd wanted a friend regardless of the difference in their families' tax brackets. Continuing that friendship had been one of Shay's very few rebellions against her father's and brother's edicts about being a Neal. She loved Bridgette like a sister, and Trevor's disapproval wouldn't make her give up her friend.

"Which reminds me," Shay continued, not giving him a chance to offer yet another opinion on her relationship with Bridgette. "I won't be able to make dinner tonight, either. I made other plans."

His gaze narrowed on her. "Dinner is with the senator, his wife and several of his friends."

"I'm aware, and I apologize for backing out at the last moment, but something came up that I can't reschedule."

She returned his stare, not offering an explanation about the "something" even though his eyes demanded one. The words actually shoved at the back of her throat, but she refused to soothe him, to cave just to keep the peace. Especially since he'd been the one to make the plans for this dinner without even checking to see if she was available. Sometimes her brother misinterpreted her silence for meekness. And sometimes she let his high-handedness go. But not when it mattered. And tonight mattered. To her.

"Shay," he murmured, leaning back in his chair, his mouth hardening even more. "I know I don't need to remind you how important the next few months are to me, to our family and, therefore, to Remington-Neal. This wedding isn't just gearing up to be the social event of next year, but it's also only months before Senator Reus's campaign kicks off. We can't afford to have anything go wrong. We're Neals, with a name and reputation above reproach. Don't do anything to taint either."

Anger at his thinly veiled admonishment surged within her, and she fought down the barrage of words blistering her throat. The same throat that constricted as the noose of the Neal name tightened, suffocating her. She'd always been the dutiful daughter, the proper socialite and, except for in her head, had done it all without complaint. But lately, the constraints were chafing, leaving her raw and irritated. In emotional pain.

Well, you haven't been that *proper.*

The same snarky voice that had taunted her about Madison mocked her again, this time following it up with a parade of vivid, explicit images of the night she'd spent with Gideon Knight. Her belly clenched, a dark swirl of desire eddying far south of her navel. Flashes of those lust-drenched hours burst in her head like fireworks across a dark July night. Gideon kneeling before her, lips glistening with the evidence of the desire he'd coaxed out of her with that same talented mouth. Gideon leaning over her, midnight hair tumbling around them, his big body moving over hers...in hers.

Gideon sleeping as she quietly dressed in the murky morning light, the sharp angles and planes of his face not softened by slumber.

Heat rushed up her chest and throat and poured into her face. She ducked her head over her plate, concealing the flush that surely stained her cheekbones.

"Shay?"

She jerked her head up, freeing herself from thoughts of Gideon. Inhaling, she refocused on their conversation. "No, I don't need to be reminded. And missing one dinner isn't going to mar the Neal name or threaten the senator's campaign," she replied. Ignoring the narrowing of his eyes, she pushed her chair back and stood. "I need to get to the office. I'll see you later."

Leaning over, she brushed a kiss across his cheek, then left the room before he could attempt to dig into her reasons for not complying with his plans. As soon as she stepped over the threshold, she heaved a sigh. The tension that seemed to be more of a common occurrence when she was with Trevor eased from her shoulders.

Shoulders that were aching from carrying the heavy burden of her brother's expectations.

Six

Shay smiled up at her server as she accepted the black folder containing the check for the meal she'd just finished. Well, a little more than a meal. Her smile widened at the warm glow of satisfaction radiating inside her chest. A business meeting with the two women who had just left the restaurant, and one that had gone extremely well.

This had been her reason for ducking out on dinner with Trevor, Madison and her family. As much as Shay's job at RemingtonNeal bored the hell out of her, she was grateful for it. Without the six-figure salary, she wouldn't be able to finance her own secret company—an investment firm that funded innovative, promising start-ups—start-ups founded by women.

Shay made it possible for women to achieve their

dreams, and with a percentage of the profits, she was able to continue growing her own business. Leida Investments—named after her mother—was hers alone, without any connection to her family. Even the incorporation documents weren't in her name. The anonymity—and the NDA she had all her clients sign—allowed her the freedom to use the degrees she'd earned without anyone trying to pigeonhole her. Yes, enduring the time she put in at her brother's company was well worth it when she could be her own boss.

If Trevor discovered her secret, he would do more than disapprove of it; he would sabotage it. As archaic as it sounded, he possessed firm ideas about her role in the family and the business. He might have created a lip service position for her at RemingtonNeal, but he intended for her to be a replica of their mother—wife, mother, philanthropist, socialite and the perfect hostess. The philanthropist part wasn't bad, but the rest of it? She mentally shuddered.

Tonight was a reminder of why she went to such measures to maintain her subterfuge. The excitement and joy that had lit Jennifer Ridland's and Marcia Brennan's faces as Shay slid an investment contract across the table had reinforced for her why her company must continue to thrive without any interference from her brother. The two women could revolutionize the travel industry, and she wanted to be the one who helped them do it.

Oh yes, this was well worth missing out on Trevor's dinner.

"Good evening, Ms. Neal. Do you mind if I join you?"

That voice. Shock blasted through her, and under it wound a current of something darker, sultrier. Her voice and breath crowded into her throat like an angry mob, strangling her for a long, panicked moment.

Even when Gideon Knight slid into the chair across from her, she remained speechless, frozen. It was as if her thoughts of him earlier that morning had conjured him. The bottomless onyx eyes no longer glittered with lust, but they held the same piercing intensity. It had her wavering between ducking her head and allowing him to pilfer her darkest secrets. The angular but beautiful face with its sharp angles and unsmiling, sinfully full lips… The tall, powerful body that seemed to dwarf the chair and table…

A shiver shuddered through her body, and she prayed he didn't notice. *What are you doing here?* almost tumbled from her lips before she hauled the words back. But recognition didn't shine in his eyes. Then, why would it? He'd spent a hot, sex-drenched night during a blackout with Camille, a member of the waitstaff. Across from him sat Shay Neal, composed heiress with long, dark brown hair instead of a wig, no glasses, hazel eyes instead of brown contacts and an eggplant-colored, long-sleeved cocktail dress instead of a uniform.

She bore no resemblance to the woman he'd known. Touched. Brought such immense pleasure.

"I'm afraid I'm just finishing up dinner, Mr…" She trailed off. God, she felt like such a hypocrite, a liar. Intentional deception wasn't her. But she couldn't confess how they knew one another, either. One, she'd lied to him about her identity. Two, if he discovered that she and Camille were the same person, he could use that to embarrass her family. If Trevor found out... She mentally shook her head. No, not an option.

"Gideon Knight," he said, setting a brown folder on the table. "And I promise not to take up too much of your time. But I believe you will want to hear what I have to say."

Though every instinct for self-preservation inside her screamed to run and run *now*, she remained seated. His almost emotionless tone didn't conceal the faint warning in his words.

And then there was the part of her—the part she struggled not to acknowledge—that trembled with desire from just being near Gideon. If she could just erase that night from her head...

"I'm sorry, Mr. Knight, but I don't know you." Not a lie. Biblical knowledge didn't equate *knowing* someone. "Therefore, I don't believe there is anything we need to speak about. So if you'll excuse me..."

She set her napkin on the table and started to rise from her chair. Yes, she was being rude, but desperation trumped manners. She needed to get away from him before she did something foolish. Such as beg him for a repeat of a night that never should've happened.

"I know your secret, Ms. Neal."

Shay froze. Except for her heart. It pounded against her sternum like an anvil against steel. Hard. Deafening.

Slowly, she lowered herself to her seat, forcing her expression into one of calm disinterest. Hiding the fear that coursed through her like a rushing current.

He knew about the night of the blackout? What had she done to betray her identity? Oh God. *What did he intend to do with the information?*

"I'm afraid I have no idea what you're talking about," she replied.

His aloof, shuttered demeanor didn't alter as he cocked his head and studied her. "Is your brother aware of where you are tonight? Does he know about the meeting you concluded just minutes ago?"

Wait. What? "I'm sorry?" she asked.

"Does he know about Leida Investments?" he clarified, leaning back in his chair. "I must admit, I can't imagine Trevor Neal supporting his sister running a company that is outside of RemingtonNeal. More specifically, out from under his control."

Equal parts relief and unease swirled in her belly. Relief because he still hadn't equated her with Camille. But unease because how did he know about her business? Better question, why did he care?

"Forgive me for not seeing how it's any of your concern," she answered, ice in her voice.

"Forgiveness. Oh, we're so far past that," he murmured, and as she frowned at the cryptic words, he slid the brown folder across the table toward her.

That sense of unease morphed into dread as she stared at the banded file. She lifted her hand, but at the last moment, she froze, her fingers hovering above it as if it were a scorpion, ready to strike and poison her with its venom.

Yet she grasped it, then opened it.

Minutes later, her heart thudded against her chest

wall like a hammer against stone. The pounding clang in her head deafened her. God, she wished it would blind her to what she was reading.

Report after report detailing shady business deals involving her brother, and even some with his future father-in-law, Senator Reus. Bribery for product placement, undercutting bidding contracts, predatory practices, procuring illegal campaign contributions on behalf of the senator. And these were just some of the accusations leveled against Trevor and RemingtonNeal.

"Why are you showing me these…these lies?" She dropped the stack back on the table as if it singed her fingertips. If it didn't betray weakness, she would've shoved her chair back from the table just to place more space between that file and her.

"Lies?" He arched a black eyebrow, the corner of his mouth lifting in the faintest of sneers. "Facts, Ms. Neal. Your determination to believe they're false doesn't make it so."

"And your determination to believe they're true doesn't make it so," she snapped, throwing his words back at him. "I don't know you, and I damn sure don't know the people who gathered this defamatory conjecture." She flicked a corner of the folder. "Let's face it, Mr. Knight. If any of this was provable in court, you wouldn't be sitting here across from me at a restaurant table. You would be meeting with the DA or SEC."

"That's where you're wrong," he said, cruel satisfaction glinting in his eyes. "It's amazing how the court of public opinion will try and convict someone much swifter than a court of law."

Her stomach rolled, bile churning before racing for the back of her throat. She hated to admit it, but he was right. Good God, if *any* of this information leaked, it would destroy Trevor's reputation, his engagement, and irreparably harm the family company. It wouldn't matter if the claims couldn't be proved; the speculation alone would be detrimental and the damage irreversible. Since their father died, Trevor's one goal—no, his obsession—had been to enlarge RemingtonNeal, to make it even more successful and powerful than what their father had done. None of that would be possible if even an iota of the data in this dossier was true.

Not that she believed it. She *couldn't*. Yes, Trevor could be merciless and cut-throat. She'd increasingly seen more and more evidence of this, personally and professionally, in the last few years. And it worried her. The glimpses of the brother she'd revered and adored as a child and teen were becoming further and further apart.

But it was those glimpses that gave her hope. That reminded her that underneath the often cold demeanor existed a good man. A man incapable of the things noted in that defaming file.

And bottom line… She loved him.

Love and loyalty demanded she believe in him.

"What do you want?" she asked, forcing a calm into her voice that was a farce. Questions, thoughts and *fear* whipped through her in a chaotic gale.

The man who'd fed her and provided her protection and light in a blackout didn't sit across from her. No, this wasn't the man who'd introduced her to such pleasure she still felt the echo of it weeks later. This man... He was a stranger. A cold, calculating, beautiful stranger.

"You."

The blunt announcement doused her in a frigid blast, stunning her.

"Excuse me?" she rasped.

He couldn't mean...?

No. No way.

He didn't want her. He had to mean something else.

But God, her body was having one hell of a time getting the message. *You.* Heat prickled at the base of her spine, and desire wound through her veins like a molten stream. A barrage of memories assaulted her—the sound of his ragged breath in her ear as he thrust into her body, all that dark, thick hair tumbling around his lust-tautened face, his whispered "moonbeam" as he stroked her damn skin... Her breath evaporated in her lungs, and she struggled to keep any hint of arousal from her face.

"I want you." He leaned forward, his midnight gaze pinning her to her chair. "More specifically, I want you to be in love with me."

The images in her head splintered like glass, dousing the passion-kindled flames inside her. She gaped at him. Couldn't help it. After all, it wasn't every day that she sat across from a lunatic.

"Are you crazy?" she demanded, clutching the edge of the table as if it were the only thing keeping her from leaping out of her chair. "I don't even *like* you. And we've never met," she continued, ignoring the memory of skin pressed to damp skin that flashed across her mind's eye. "How could you believe you love me?"

He flicked a hand, the gesture impatient, dismissive. "Of course I don't love you. And I don't need your affection or professions of an emotion that is nothing but an excuse for fools and liars to behave badly."

Shay shook her head, confused. "But you just said—"

"Pretend," he interrupted. "You're going to pretend to be deeply enamored with me, and our whirlwind relationship will be as fake as that sentiment."

"You *are* crazy," she breathed. "That's ridiculous. Why would you even propose something like that?"

"Why?" he repeated, that damn eyebrow arching again. "Your brother."

She barked out a harsh crack of laughter. "My brother? Do you really think Trevor cares if I'm in a relationship with you?" Hell, he might be happy. Yes, he and Gideon were business rivals, and Trevor had been trying to acquire the other man's company for years, but her brother would probably consider it a coup for his sister to date such a successful and wealthy man.

But for the first time since sitting down across from her, Gideon smiled. The curling of his sensual lips was slow, deliberate…and menacing. "Oh yes. Your brother will care. And he'll understand."

"Another enigmatic message, Mr. Knight?" She waved a hand, frustrated. "I'm too old for games. Whatever your play is here, make it plain."

"I'll make this very plain, Shay," he said, using her given name even though she hadn't granted him permission to do so. His voice, as dark and sinful as his eyes, caressed her name like a long, luxurious stroke. It was damn near indecent.

"You can pretend to be my significant other, and convince your brother that you are mine. Or…" a steely edge that was both lethally sharp and smooth entered his voice "…I can let the truth about Leida Investments drop into your brother's lap. Imagine his fury when he realizes the secrets his sister has been keeping. And then, while that little bomb detonates, I will release the information in that file to not just the SEC but to every news outlet and journalist I have access to. And believe me, the list is long. As would be the jail sentences your brother and his precious senator would face for everything they've been up to. What effect do you think the meltdown of your family name and company will have? How many people will want to accept funds from a woman associated with a man whose name will be synonymous with financial scandal and fraud? Even the desperate will think twice about that. So both of you would be ruined, if everything in that dossier leaks. That leaves us at an impasse, Shay."

He paused, and the import of his words—no, his *threat*—sank into her like the realization of a floundering person being swallowed by quicksand.

Slow but no escape.

"And the choice is yours."

Seven

Gideon inhaled as he entered his mother's Lincoln Park home, and the sense of calm that always settled on him when he was with his family wrapped around him like a warm embrace.

Though his mother and sister had lived in the six-bedroom, seven-bathroom home for only four years, it was home because they were there. It was as much his sanctuary as his own downtown Chicago condominium. As the sound of his mother and Pat Benatar singing about love being a battlefield on her ever-present radio reached him, he shook his head, amending his thought. No, it was *more* of a haven for him.

Because family was *everything*.

Striding past the formal living and dining rooms with their soaring twelve-foot ceilings, and the sweeping, curving staircase, he headed toward the rear of the house. His mother might have initially balked at him purchasing this home for her and Olivia in one of Chicago's wealthiest neighborhoods, but there'd never been any doubt about how much she adored the airy, state-of-the-art kitchen. With its wall of windows, restaurant-style ranges and cooktops, top-of-the-line appliances, large marble island and butcher block and dual workhorse sinks, Ai had instantly fallen in love. And it was in this room that he usually found her.

Like now.

Ai stood at the stove, still clothed in her professor outfit—elegant gray pantsuit with crimson blouse and hair in a loose bun at the nape of her neck—and barefoot. Her slim body swayed back and forth to the eighties' rock anthem, and Gideon stifled a snort as she perfectly executed an arm-and-hip dance move he recognized from the classic MTV video.

He gave her a slow clap.

She whirled around with a gasp, brandishing a tea strainer like a club. "*Gideon,*" she scolded, splaying the fingers of her free hand over her chest. "Are you trying to give me a heart attack?" She replaced the strainer in the waiting cup of steaming water and shot him a look over her shoulder. "I warn you, if I go, all of my money has been left to your grandmother's Maltese puppy."

Chuckling, he crossed the room and pulled his mother into a hug. Her familiar scent of gardenias greeted him like a childhood friend. Only with his family could he be Gideon Jian Knight, the oldest son of Ai Knight, former cafeteria worker who busted her ass to provide for her children and earn her PhD in educational studies at the same time. With them, he could lower the guards he'd erected between him and the rest of the world, especially those who greedily grasped for money, connections, time or sex from Gideon Knight, CEO of KayCee Corp.

He jealously guarded his moments with his family. Zealously protected *them*.

"That's fine," he assured her, with a quick kiss to her forehead. "I have the very best legal department, and they would be capable of breaking that will." He smiled as she swatted at him. But then he noted the two cups on the gleaming countertop, and his amusement faded. "How is she?" he murmured.

The light in his mother's eyes dimmed. "Better," she answered. She sighed, turning back to preparing the hot tea. "She's still sleeping more than I like and hasn't left the house since coming home from the hospital a week and a half ago. But…better." She checked the strainer in the second cup. "I was just about to take this up and sit with her for a while."

"I can do that, Mom. You obviously just arrived home." She didn't have to continue to work as a social sciences and history professor at the University of Chicago. He was more than willing to provide for her, as she'd done for him and Olivia. But Ai Knight wouldn't hear of it, and Gideon was proud to have one of the most loved professors at U of C as his mother. "Go upstairs, relax and I'll take care of Livvie."

"Thank you." She turned, smiling softly and extending her hands toward him. He enfolded hers in his, squeezing them. "But no, I want to spend some time with her before I grade papers. Although she always loves to hear you play. Maybe you could bring your guitar by sometime this week."

"I'll do that," he agreed.

His mother had been responsible for him first picking up the instrument. She'd found a battered acoustic Fender at a garage sale, and from the second he'd held it, he'd been enamored. Though extra money had been almost nonexistent during his childhood, she'd still found a way to pay for lessons. No one outside the family had ever heard him play, because it was for him. His peace. His way to lose himself and get away from the stresses of running a multimillion-dollar tech company.

Ai cupped his cheek, giving it an affectionate pat before lowering her arm. "Now, not that I don't enjoy you dropping by, but is everything okay?"

"Yes. There's something I do need to speak with you about, though." He propped a hip against the island and crossed his arms over his chest.

She studied him, then nodded, copying his pose. "Okay. What's going on?"

"I had a...business meeting last night," he said. "With Shay Neal. Trevor Neal's sister."

Surprise widened his mother's eyes. "I didn't even know he had a sister," she whispered, then shook her head. "Why, Gideon? What could you possibly have to discuss with her?"

"Our common interest," he said. "Her brother."

"Gideon," she murmured, tilting her head to the side. "What did you do?"

Meeting his mother's gaze, he relayed his conversation with Shay, including his revelation of all he'd dug up on Trevor, the ultimatum he'd delivered and her refusal to give him an answer.

"What are you thinking, son?" she asked, worry crowding her gaze. "She's innocent in all this."

Innocent. His fingers curled around his biceps, tightening even as blood pumped hot and fast through his body. *Innocent* was one word he wouldn't have associated with Shay Neal.

He'd done his homework on her before ambushing her at the restaurant. Twenty-five years old. Graduated with honors from Loyola University's Quinlan School of Business with a bachelor's in finance and entrepreneurship and a master of business administration. A member of Women in Business and International Business Society. Currently worked as vice president of the Social Development department at Remington-Neal. And from what he could tell, the position was nothing but a fancy term for event coordinator, and definitely underutilized the education she'd received. All this information could be found on her social network platforms or the company's website.

Only a deeper dive below the surface uncovered her ownership of Leida Investments. The degrees and obvious intelligence had made her interesting. But this— the company she owned in secrecy—fascinated him. This society princess who organized brunches and galas was a mystery wrapped in an enigma. And anything he couldn't dissect and analyze he mistrusted. Tack onto that her last name, and he wouldn't dare to blink around her, vigilant of the knife that might slide into his back in that flick of time.

Still…nothing, not his caution, his preparation or even the pictures included in his private investigator's file, could've prepared him for the impact of Shay Neal face-to-face.

His grandmother owned an antique locket that she'd brought with her from China. Inside was a black-and-white picture of her older sister, who'd died in childbirth. In the image, his great-aunt had been composed, stoic. But in her lovely features—in her eyes—there glimmered emotion, vitality. *Life.* It emanated through the aloof expression like dawn breaking through the last, clinging shadows of night.

And staring at Shay Neal had been like gazing upon that faded photo. Yes, she was gorgeous. No one could deny she was beautiful—the refined bone structure with high, proud cheekbones, the patrician nose with its flared nostrils, or the full curves of a mouth that belonged on a pin-up model and not a demure socialite. And he couldn't deny that just for a moment, his wayward, rebellious mind had wondered if her gleaming golden brown skin was as butter-soft as it appeared.

But it'd been none of those features that had drawn him. Fueled an insane impulse to drag his chair closer and discover what scent rose from the corner where neck and shoulder met. Had his fingers itching to pluck the strings of his guitar and find the melody that would encapsulate her.

No, it was the intelligence, the spark, the *fire* in those arresting hazel eyes.

It made him mistrust her even more.

And then there was the niggling sense of familiarity that had hit him the moment he'd sat down at her table. As if they'd met before… But like he'd done last night, he dismissed the feeling. If he'd ever met Shay Neal, no way in hell he wouldn't remember.

"She's a Neal, Mom," he said, shoving thoughts of her—of the unsettling effect she had on him—away. "She doesn't have clean hands."

"That's probably the same logic Trevor employed when he went after your sister," she pointed out, and the words struck him in the chest, burrowing into his heart.

"I'm nothing like him," he ground out, lowering his arms and curling his fingers around the edge of the marble top. "He stalked Livvie, lied to her, used her, then tossed her aside like yesterday's trash. I've been completely up-front with Shay, laying my intentions out and offering her a choice. Trevor stole Livvie's choice from her." He broke off, tipping his head back and deliberately cooling his rising temper. "You might not agree with my methods, and I'm sorry for that. But I didn't do anything when he damn near broke my sister, because you both asked me not to. I can't let it go this time. I'm not going to allow Trevor Neal to continue mistreating women. By the time I'm finished with him, he will have nothing left, and no woman will fall victim to him again."

It was the guilt that drove him.

Because it was his fault Trevor had sought out Olivia in the first place. If not for their mutual hatred and ongoing feud, she would've been safe.

"Gideon." His mother shifted forward, once more cupping his cheek. "You're right. I don't agree with your methods. I believe they will more than likely backfire, and not only will an innocent woman be hurt, but you will, too, son. If you have a conscience—which I know you do—there's no way you can't be affected by this path. And I wish you would end it now before this goes too far." She sighed, her gaze searching his. "But I also know you. And from the moment you refused to be born on your due date, I figured out you're stubborn. I'm not going to change your mind, I get that. So just…please. Be careful."

"Don't worry about me. I have everything under control," he assured her, hugging her close.

She didn't reply, instead squeezed him tighter.

He hated disappointing her, but nothing, *nothing* could dissuade him from his plans. Not her disapproval. Not Shay's reluctance and refusal to give him a decision.

He had one purpose. To bring down Trevor Neal.

And hell couldn't stop him from accomplishing it.

Eight

"Trevor, the gala is a wonderful success. You should be proud. I'm certain your parents would be," Senator Julian Reus praised, pumping his future son-in-law's hand.

I don't know how you can say that, since you never met either of them.

Shay mentally winced over the snarky comment echoing in her head. God, she really wanted to like the influential man who would soon be part of her family. But he was such a…politician. Charming. Affable.

And phony.

Good thing she never voted for him.

"Thank you, sir." Trevor smiled, then slid an arm around Shay's shoulders. "I wish I could take the credit, but it belongs to Shay. She's the reason we've already surpassed the donations from last year."

Pride glowed like an ember in her chest, and for the first time that evening, a genuine smile curled her lips.

"Thank you, Trev," she said, wrapping an arm around his waist and briefly squeezing.

"Next year, it'll be even more of a success, with Madison by your side. I'm sure she will be more than happy to step in and help organize this special event." Senator Reus announced his daughter's involvement in Grace Sanctuary as a foregone conclusion.

"Of course I will, Daddy," Madison agreed, tilting her head back expectantly, and Trevor obliged her with a soft, quick kiss on the lips. "Shay and I will make a wonderful team."

Madison turned that wide smile to Shay, and even though all the warmth that had filled her faded away, Shay returned it with one of her own.

Trevor's fiancée had been nothing but cordial to Shay, but again, there was something not quite genuine about her. Madison reminded Shay of the ice sculpture in the lobby outside the ballroom. Beautiful but cold. To stand too close would send a shiver through the body.

"Let's get through tonight first before thinking about next year," Shay said, not committing to anything. Trevor stiffened beside her, but she ignored the telltale sign of his irritation. Her mind jumped to that dark brown file Gideon Knight had slid across the table. She thought about how her brother donated significant funds to the senator's campaign. And she couldn't help but wonder if some of that money came from their mother's organization.

Stop it.

The sharp order ricocheted off her skull. Damn Gideon Knight. She hated that he'd infiltrated her head, and she couldn't evict him. Not his damn dossier or the man himself. It'd been four days since that meeting—no, ambush. Four days since she was supposed to give him her decision about his preposterous ultimatum.

Four nights of heated fantasies that left her twisting and aching in her bed.

What kind of sister did it make her that she woke up shaking and hungry for the man who blackmailed her? Who threatened her brother's livelihood and freedom?

A sad excuse for one.

Smothering a sigh, she excused herself from their small group on the pretense of checking with the catering staff, and headed across the room. She'd taken only a dozen steps before tingles jangled up her bare arms and culminated at the nape of her neck.

She sucked in a breath and immediately scanned the crowded ballroom for the source of the unsettling, *exciting* feeling.

There. No...*there.*

Gideon Knight.

The unexpected sight of him glued her feet to the floor.

Unexpected? Really?

Okay, maybe not. As soon as that prickle had sizzled over her skin, a part of her had instinctively known who'd caused it. Only one man had ever had that kind of effect on her.

She stared at him, trapped in an instant of déjà vu. Seeing him in his black tuxedo, she was swept back to the first night they'd met. Once more he seemed like the imposing but regal warlord surveying his subjects, his armor traded for perfectly tailored formal wear, his hair emphasizing the stark but gorgeous lines of his face. The distance of the ballroom separated them, but she somehow sensed those black eyes on her, just like then.

Just like then, she fought the dual urges of fight or flight.

And by fight she meant the warring of their mouths and bodies for dominance.

Damn.

She balled her fist, forcing her feet to maintain a steady, unhurried pace forward. Even as her heart pounded a relentless rhythm against her sternum.

"How did you get in here?" she gritted out.

Conscious of any gazes that might be leveled on them, she kept her polite, social mask in place, when in truth she wanted to glare daggers at him.

His aloof expression didn't change...except for the arch of that damnable dark eyebrow. "I expect like everyone else. The front entrance. And paying the seven-thousand-dollar-a-plate fee."

"That's not possible," she snapped. "I looked over and approved the final guest list myself. Neither you nor your company's name was on it."

"Then you missed it. Maybe other matters distracted you," he added. A beat of charged silence vibrated between them. No need to name the "other matters." They both were well aware of what he referred to.

"Is that why you're here?" she demanded, and in spite of her resolve, her voice dropped to a heated whisper. "To pressure me for an answer?"

"It's been four days, Shay," he replied, and in that moment, she resented his carefully modulated composure.

The rash and admittedly foolish urge—no, *need*—to shatter his control swelled within her. She wanted the man from the blackout, the one who stared at her with flames of desire burning in his onyx eyes as he drove them both to impossible pleasure.

"I've given your four days longer than I'd usually grant anyone else."

"Well, I'm flattered."

"You should be."

She clenched her teeth so hard an ache rose along her jaw. "The answer is n—"

"Is this man bothering you, Shay?" Trevor appeared at her elbow, and both the venom in his question and his sudden, hard grasp elicited a gasp from her.

Gideon's gaze dropped to her arm, and anger narrowed his eyes.

"Get your hand off of her," he ordered. The volume of his voice didn't rise, but only a simpleton could miss the warning. "You're hurting her."

Scowling, Trevor glanced down at his fingers pinching her arm, then jerked his hand away. He lifted his regard to her face, and she glimpsed disgust, but also regret. She dipped her chin in a silent acknowledgment of his equally silent apology.

Turning back to Gideon, he snarled, "What are you doing here? You weren't invited. Leave. Now."

"I'm afraid that's not going to happen," Gideon said, with no hint of remorse. If anything, satisfaction rang loud and clear in those words. "I paid to attend just like everyone else here, and made a hefty donation on top of that. I'm staying."

"You can have your money back. We don't need it," Trevor spat, nearly trembling with rage as he edged closer to Gideon. "We both know why you're here. You lost. Get over it. It's not like it's the first time, and it damn sure won't be the last."

Fear spiked inside Shay's chest. *Good God.* She'd never seen her brother this angry. His reaction to Gideon's presence had to be more than a business rivalry. This was…personal.

"Trevor," she quietly pleaded, gently but firmly grasping his arm. "Please."

Gideon shifted his attention from her brother to her. And the same fury that twisted her brother's face lit his eyes like a glittering night sky. But as he studied her, some of the anger dimmed.

He retreated a step, his gaze still pinned on her.

Shock pummeled the breath from her lungs. Had he backed away…for her?

No. That was impossible. He didn't give a damn about her or her feelings.

Still…

"Have a nice evening. Both of you," he said, though

his regard never wavered from her. "It was wonderful seeing you again, Shay," he murmured, then turned and headed farther into the room, not toward the exit as Trevor had demanded.

"What was he talking about, 'seeing you again'?" Trevor hissed as soon as Gideon was out of earshot. "When did you meet him?"

With Herculean effort, she tore her gaze from Gideon and met her brother's glare. Hurt and hints of betrayal lurked there. And guilt pricked her. For what, though? She'd done nothing wrong.

"A few nights ago when I had dinner with friends. He was at the same restaurant." She delivered the half-truth with aplomb. *God, when did I become such an accomplished liar?* "He just introduced himself, that was all. What in the world was that all about, Trevor?"

"Nothing," he snapped. Then, sighing, he dragged a hand over his closely cropped hair. "I'm sorry. I didn't mean to bark at you. Just…stay away from him, Shay. I don't want you to have anything to do with him. Do you understand?"

"I'm not a child, Trevor," she murmured, meeting his fierce stare. "And this isn't the proper place for this discussion, either. We have guests."

With that reminder, she turned and strode away from him and the disturbing scene that had just unfolded.

Oh yes, there was bad blood between him and Gideon. Now more than ever, she felt like a pawn in whatever twisted game the two of them were engaged in. And she hated it.

As the evening progressed, she couldn't uproot the bitterness. Maintaining her not-a-care-in-the-world socialite persona became a weightier burden, and by the time dinner was being cleared away, she was bone-deep exhausted. Peeking at the slim, gold watch on her wrist, she thanked God she had only about an hour more to do her hostess duty before she could escape.

"I noticed you talking to Gideon Knight earlier," Madison said, her tone low enough that Trevor, who was engrossed in conversation with Senator Reus, didn't overhear.

Surprised that she knew of him, Shay nodded. "Yes."

"Do you know him well?" she asked, and unease niggled at Shay. The air of nonchalance in Madison's seemingly innocent question seemed forced.

"Not really," Shay replied cautiously. "Though Trevor seems to."

"Oh, you don't know, do you?" Madison studied her, a gleam in her dark brown eyes. "Trevor didn't tell you?" she prodded before Shay could answer. "Gideon and I were…close before I met your brother."

"Close," Shay repeated, though the twisting in her stomach interpreted the coy choice of phrasing.

"Engaged, actually," Madison confessed, and this time, there was no mistaking the cat-that-ate-the-whole-damn-flock-of-canaries smile that curved her mouth. "We were engaged for a year before we ended our relationship. He wasn't happy about it." She chuckled, apparently amused at her understatement.

We both know why you're here. You lost. Get over

*it. It's not like it's the first time, and it damn sure won't
be the last.*

Trevor's accusation echoed in her head, and it now
made sickening sense. As did Gideon's reason about
why he'd proposed his ridiculous plan, that night at
the restaurant.

Your brother, he'd said. All of this—hatred, blackmail, rivalry—was over a woman.

Her belly lurched, and she fisted her fingers, willing the coq au vin she'd just eaten not to make a re-
appearance.

"If I may have your attention, please?" Senator Reus
stood, his booming politician's voice carrying through
the ballroom and silencing the after-dinner chatter.

"Thank you. Now I know this evening is about
Grace Sanctuary, and I speak on behalf of both the
Reus and Neal families when I thank you for your gen-
erosity in both spirit and donations." Applause rose,
and Julian Reus basked in it, his smile benevolent.
No, the evening wasn't about him, but somehow, he'd
managed to make it all about him.

"I'd just like to take this moment to recognize this
wonderful charity, as well as Trevor Neal, who has
spearheaded it since the passing of his dear parents.
I'm so proud that I will be able to call him son in
the very near future, as he and my beautiful daughter, Madison, embark on a journey together as man
and wife. Trevor…" he accepted a glass of champagne
from a waiter who suddenly appeared at his elbow, and
lifted it high "…congratulations to you and my daugh-

ter. You are the son I wasn't blessed with, but am so fortunate to now have."

Around them, people hoisted their own wine-glasses and echoed "To Trevor," as her brother stood and clasped the senator's hand, his huge grin so blinding, Shay had to glance away. The sight of him soaking up the senator's validation like water on parched earth caused pain to shudder through her.

Their father would've never praised him so publicly—or privately. Lincoln Neal had been a hard man, huge on demands and criticism, and stingy with compliments. She, more than anyone, understood how Trevor had craved his approval. And it'd been their father's refusal to give it that had changed Trevor. Their father had been dead for five years, and Trevor still drove himself to be the best...to be better than their father. This high regard from such an important man had to be like Christmas to Trevor. A thousand of them packed into one short toast.

Oh God. She dipped her head so no one could glimpse the sting of tears in her eyes.

She was going to cave to Gideon's ultimatum.

Family. Loyalty.

Those were the tenets that had been drilled into them from childhood. Definitely by their father, and even in one of the last conversations she'd had with her mother before she died. She'd stressed that Shay and Trevor always take care of one another.

Family loyalty wouldn't allow her to let Trevor lose everything. The family name. His company. His fiancée. His future father-in-law. There was no one left to protect him, except her. And until she could verify the truth of the information Gideon held—and she still doubted the veracity of it, especially given what she'd learned from Madison—she couldn't permit her brother to be ruined. Not when the kind but wounded boy she remembered still existed inside him.

He was her brother.

And to keep that happiness shining on her brother's face, she would make a deal with the devil.

And Gideon Knight was close enough.

It wasn't difficult to locate him in the crowded room. The entire evening she'd been aware of his presence, and when she glanced over her shoulder to the table several feet away, their gazes immediately locked. As if he'd only been waiting for her to look his way.

She gave him a small nod, and he returned it.

Exhaling, she turned her attention to the glass of red wine she'd barely touched throughout dinner. Now it, and about four more, seemed like a fabulous idea.

She would need all the courage she could get.

Nine

"When I agreed to meet you, I assumed we would go to another restaurant, not your home."

Gideon stepped down into the recessed living room of his downtown Chicago penthouse and slipped his hands into the pockets of his tuxedo pants. Shay hovered at the top of the two steps leading into the room.

He surveyed his home, attempting to view it through her eyes. The dual-level, four-bedroom, three-bath condominium was the epitome of luxury with its airy, open-floor plan, floor-to-ceiling windows, game and media rooms, indoor and outdoor kitchens and private rooftop lounge that boasted its own fireplace. But it'd been the stunning views of the Chicago River and Chicago skyline from every room that had sold him. It was like being a part of the elements while protected from them.

He'd left most of the simple, elegant decor to his interior designer, but scattered among the gray, white and black color scheme were pieces of him, if Shay cared to look close enough. Next to the god-awful piece of metallic abstract art on the fireplace mantel that he'd never gotten around to tossing stood a framed photo of him with his family, including his grandparents, at last year's Mid-Autumn Festival in Chinatown.

On top of the white baby grand piano where his sister sometimes plucked out "Mary Had a Little Lamb" sat the guitar pick he'd forgotten to put away the night before.

Peeking from between the couch pillows was the ear of a pair of Bluetooth headphones that he used to listen to music with while working from home.

Yes, if she paid attention, she might glimpse those hints into him. And part of him tensed with the need to go through the room and remove those clues from her sight. But the other half… That half wanted her to spy them, to ask questions. Which was bullshit, since their arrangement didn't require that kind of intimacy.

He shouldn't hunger for that—especially not from her. Not just sister to his enemy, but another beautiful woman who didn't want the real him. The last time he'd allowed a woman to enter into the space reserved for family, she'd betrayed that trust. Had left him so disillusioned, he'd vowed to never be that foolhardy, that reckless, again.

Only family could be trusted. Only family deserved his loyalty…his love.

Definitely not Trevor Neal's sister.

"This kind of conversation deserves more privacy than a crowded restaurant," he said, finally addressing her complaint. "Would you like a drink? Wine? Champagne? Water?"

"Champagne?" she scoffed, stepping down into the living room. "I guess this would be a victory celebration for you. But no. I'll take a Scotch. This situation calls for something strong that tastes worse than the deal I'm about to swallow."

Her acerbic retort had an inappropriate spurt of amusement curling in his chest. He squelched it, turning to fix her a finger of Scotch and a bourbon for him. Moments later, he handed the tumbler to her and silently watched as she sipped the potent liquor. Not even a flinch. His admiration grew.

When she lifted those beautiful hazel eyes to him, that niggling sense of familiarity tugged at him again. He cocked his head to the side, studying her. What was it…?

"Can we get this started, please?" she asked, setting the glass on the small table flanking the sofa. She rubbed her bare arms, and the sign of nerves pricked a conscience he'd believed to be impervious. "I'm sure you've already guessed that I'm going to agree to your ridiculous plan. Or let's just call it what it is. Extortion."

"You have a choice, Shay," he reminded her, sipping his bourbon.

"Yes," she agreed, bitterness coating the word. "Sacrifice myself or my brother to the beast. That's a hell of a choice."

He shrugged. "But one, nonetheless."

"You're not really this cold and unfeeling. I know you're not," she whispered, her green-and-amber gaze roaming his face as if trying to peer beneath the mask he chose to let her see.

Unbidden, the night of the blackout wavered in his mind. No. Those dark, hungry hours had proved he wasn't cold or unfeeling. For a rare instant, he'd lost the control he was much lauded for. But those circumstances had been extreme, and she wasn't a hardworking, passionate and fiery server named Camille. That woman had disappeared without a trace, filling in for another member of the waitstaff, and not leaving behind a hint of her identity. She'd seen the man he rarely let anyone see.

One Shay would never witness.

"If you need to make up an idea of who I am in order to fulfill the pretense of falling in love with me, then go ahead. Whatever will allow you to deliver an award-winning performance for your brother and everyone else watching."

"Everyone else being Madison Reus."

The accusation punched him in the chest, and he braced himself against the impact. By sheer will he forced himself not to react. But inside…inside he snarled at the mention of *her*. The woman who'd taught him that love could be bought by the highest bidder. Who'd knowingly betrayed him with the one man he hated. Who'd shown him that placing his heart and trust in a person outside of family was a costly mistake—to his bank account and to his soul.

He would never repeat that particular mistake.

"You must have loved her very much to go to such lengths for your revenge," Shay continued when he remained silent. "That's what this is all about, right? How dare my brother date the woman you were once engaged to? You're punishing both of them by flaunting me in their faces?"

He caught the threads of hurt beneath that calm tone. And in spite of his resolve to maintain his distance, both emotionally and physically, he shifted forward. She didn't retreat, but instead tilted her head back to meet his gaze. Courageous. He hadn't been expecting that from her.

Just like he hadn't been expecting this inconvenient attraction. Even now, her scent—the fresh, wild lushness of rain right before a storm and roses in bloom—called to him like a siren's lure, urging him closer, until his hard, solid planes pressed against her soft, sensual curves.

Though all common sense railed at him not to touch, he ignored it and reached for the thick strands of hair that fell in a sleek glide behind her shoulders. Pinching a lock between his fingers, he lifted it, indulged himself and brushed it over his lips.

Never breaking his stare, he murmured, "You don't know what you're talking about."

He heard the slight catch of her breath. Noticed the erratic beat of her pulse at the base of her neck. From nerves? Desire? The hardening of his body telegraphed which one it voted for.

Step back. Remember the plan. Stick to the plan.

But he stayed. Playing with sin-wrapped-in-bronzed-skin fire.

"No?" she breathed, the corner of her mouth lifting in a sardonic smile. "Is this the part where I just blindly trust what you say because my lying eyes and lil' ol' brain can't possibly grasp the intricacies involved here?" She scoffed, jerking her head back, and he released her. "Please. I'm patted on the head and patronized every day, so forgive me if I call bullshit."

She turned away from him, and he ground his teeth together, his fingers curling into his palms to battle the urge to grab her and bring her back against him. She didn't understand. This wasn't about Madison; it was about another woman—his sister. And that bastard who'd abused her heart and shattered her mental state.

An eye for an eye. A sister for a sister.

But he couldn't admit any of that to her. Not when she would no doubt run back and tell Trevor everything.

"You're forgetting I know the secret about your job. And I don't mean that joke of a title at Remington-Neal. I would be a fool to underestimate you, Shay."

She pivoted and something flashed in her hazel eyes, but before he could decipher it, she briefly closed them and pinched the bridge of her nose.

"Can we just get this over with?" she asked, weariness coating her voice. "Tell me what you need from me so you won't burn my brother's world to the ground."

"Like I told you at the restaurant. You and I will pretend to be a couple. A real couple, Shay. Which means convincing everyone that we're hopelessly in love." He couldn't prevent the bitter smile from curving his mouth. "I read that you took several drama classes in college. Time to dust off those old skills and bring them out of retirement. I'll require you to attend several events and dinners with me, and the same for you. The first time you try to twist out of this arrangement, it's off, and your brother's dirty dealings become public."

This time he clearly interpreted the emotion turning her gaze more green than brown. Anger. "Don't worry about me. I'll hold up my end of the bargain. But I won't carry this lie on indefinitely. You have a time limit of six months. That's all I'll agree to."

Six months would be more than enough time to carry out all he had planned. "Fine."

"And at the conclusion, you promise to destroy the report and all copies of it."

He nodded again, although he had no intention of doing that. Only a fool would reveal his hand. Did he feel a twinge of guilt for deceiving her? Yes, it didn't sit well. But he'd meant what he'd told his mother. His number one goal was to prevent Trevor from ever hurting another woman as he'd hurt Olivia. This arrangement with Shay was only one part of his plan.

"Okay, then." Shay inhaled a breath and tilted her chin up at a haughty angle, every inch the socialite. "One more thing. I'm not a whore. We might have to pretend affection for each other, but I won't have sex with you."

Irritation flashed inside him, and he took a step toward her before he drew to an abrupt halt. "I can promise you that when I take a woman to my bed, she wants to be there. I don't give a damn about love, because there's something much more honest—fucking. There are no lies when a woman is coming for me, and I don't want one in my bed who doesn't want to be there. If she can't give me the truth of her pleasure, then I don't want her under me. And any man who's satisfied with just getting a woman between the sheets, without giving a damn about her desire to be there, isn't a man."

Silence plummeted into the room, and that sense of déjà vu hit him again. He'd said something similar to Camille weeks ago when she'd accused him of using his position of power to screw her. He shook his head. He had to stop thinking about her. He couldn't afford to show any weakness or distraction around Shay.

"But you need to understand one thing, Shay, and come to terms with it." He moved forward again, lowering his head so their mouths were inches apart. So close he glimpsed the golden striations in her eyes and inhaled the heady scent of Scotch on her breath. "I'm not the other men you might have had dancing to your tune. For the next six months, you're mine. And while you might not be in my bed," he murmured, brushing the back of his finger over a sculpted cheekbone, "you'll act like you are. Which means you'll pretend to desire my touch, my hands on you. You'll behave as if you crave what I, and only I, can give you. Pleasure. Passion. A hunger so deep you don't know how you ever existed without me to take care of it for you. So, moonbeam, even if you loathe me, those beautiful eyes better convince everyone that I'm yours. And *you're mine*."

She wrenched away from him, stumbling backward, her panting audible testimony to the arousal that stained her cheeks and glinted in her eyes.

Fuck.

Need gripped his stomach, grinding and squeezing like a vise. He'd overplayed his hand. His aim had been to teach her a lesson, and he'd ended up the student with his knuckles rapped.

"Don't call me that," she ordered hoarsely. He frowned, at first not grasping what she meant. Then it hit him. Moonbeam.

Where had that come from? Why had he called her *that* name?

"Pet names, like we're something we're clearly not, aren't part of this, either." She tugged her shoulders back, and that delicate but stubborn chin went up again. "And for the record. I belong to *me*. Not my brother. Not RemingtonNeal. And definitely *not you*."

Shay spun around. Snatching up her coat, which he'd laid over the back of the foyer chair when they'd entered the penthouse, she strode out of his home.

He stood there, staring at the closed door, and a small smile played on his lips.

Whether she realized it or not, she'd just issued a challenge.

Accepted.

And he more than looked forward to winning.

Ten

Shay grimaced at the vibration of her cell phone in her back pocket as she served up an order of green papaya salad and tom yum to another hungry customer standing outside Bridgette's food truck. Her best friend's delicious Thai cuisine made hers one of the more popular trucks stationed at Hyde Park during the lunch hour.

Bridgette was a wonderful chef, and when she'd proposed starting a food truck business, Shay had insisted on investing. The love of food and cooking were just a couple things the two of them bonded over. And because they were such good friends, when Bridgette had called this morning, frantic because she'd been down a person, Shay had been more than willing to jump in and help. It hadn't been the first time she'd volunteered, and if Bridgette needed her, it wouldn't be the last. Just another reason Trevor resented her "lowbrow" relationship with Bridgette.

Good thing that she'd never told him about cooking and serving on her food truck.

Another insistent buzz of her cell, and she sighed. She knew who was calling her.

Gideon.

He'd left a message about joining him for lunch about a half hour after Bridgette's panicked call. She'd shot a text off to him, letting him know meeting wouldn't be possible. But had he accepted that? Hell no. Well, that fell under the category of His Problem.

Yes, she'd agreed to attend events with him, but she'd also meant it when she told him he didn't own her. She was more than willing to accompany him to dinners, lunches, parties, whatever. But she also needed notice, and not just a couple hours. She had a life and refused to hand it over to him.

She was already an indentured servant to the Neal name and reputation. He wouldn't become another master.

You're mine.

Those two words had played over and over in her head like a rabid hamster in a wheel. It'd been two days since she'd left his penthouse, and she hadn't been able to erase the declaration from her mind.

Or deny the spark of desire that had erupted into a conflagration inside her. Her thighs had clenched at the dark, sensual note so dominant in his voice. And in that moment, she swore she could feel the heavy, thrilling possession of his body taking hers, filling hers.

Claiming hers.

God, it wasn't fair. Not the words he uttered to her. Not the out-of-control reaction of her body to his.

She didn't have to pretend to know his touch. No, she had intimate knowledge of it.

Which was why she'd reacted so strongly—and unwisely—to the "moonbeam" he'd so carelessly tossed at her. That endearment had been special to her, meant for her alone. But it hadn't been. God only knew how many women he'd said it to.

She wasn't special.

And damn, that had hurt. More than it should've.

Another buzz, and she gritted her teeth. Probably a threatening message this time. The tenacity that had made him so successful as a businessman was working the hell out of her nerves.

Six months. She just had to hold on for six months. Then she would be free. From both this "agreement" with Gideon and from under the yoke of the Neal name.

Gideon didn't know the significance of her time limit. In that time, she would turn twenty-six and be in control of the trust funds from her mother and maternal grandmother. With that came financial independence. She wouldn't need her paychecks from RemingtonNeal to help finance Leida Investments. With the money from her trust funds, she would have more than enough capital, and while she wouldn't totally be able to escape the assumptions because of her last name, she would no longer be under the restrictions and expectations of her brother and her family reputation.

From birth, she'd been under a man's thumb: her father's, her brother's and now Gideon's.

In just six months, she would be liberated from them all.

"Here you go, babe." Bridgette handed her an order of pad thai, disrupting her thoughts of emancipation. "That's number 66."

"Thanks." Shay accepted it, bagged it and carried it to the window. "Here you go." She passed the food to the customer with a smile and turned to the next person in line. "Hi, how can I—"

Oh hell.

Gideon.

Her eyes widened as she stared at his cold, harsh expression. "What are you doing here?" she asked, and in spite of the "you don't own me" speech she'd just delivered to herself, apprehension quivered through her at the anger glittering in his gaze.

"Wasting my time hunting you down, apparently," he ground out. "You're already reneging on our arrangement, and it hasn't even been two days. I warned you about thinking I would dance—"

"Hey, man, order and move on. Some of us have to get back to work," someone yelled from in back of Gideon. And when several more grumbles of agreement followed, Gideon whipped his head around. Immediately, the mumbling ceased.

Good Lord. That was some superpower.

He returned his attention to her and in spite of his glare, she hiked her chin up. "I'm helping a friend out. She needed me today."

His gaze narrowed further, and he growled, "Open the door."

Before she could reply, he stalked off and disappeared. But seconds later, a hard rap at the side door echoed in the truck. From the grill, Bridgette tossed her a "what the hell?" look, and, bemused, Shay shrugged and unlocked it.

The door jerked open, and Gideon strode through it. His big body and intense presence seemed to shrink the interior to that of a toy truck.

Bridgette stared at him, openmouthed and struck silent. Which wasn't an easy feat. With sharp movements, he jerked off his coat and suit jacket and hung them on a wall hook. Then he rolled his sleeves up to his elbows and pinned both her and Bridgette with that dark glare.

"Well?" he snapped. "Where do you need me?"

Need him? What was happening?

Bridgette recovered first. "Can you cook?" At his abrupt nod, she handed him a knife. "You get an order of cashew chicken going, and I'll get the green curry."

Without a word, he crossed to the sink, washed his hands, then accepted the utensil and started chopping fresh vegetables and chicken like a pro. Bridgette again shot her a look, but Shay shrugged, still stunned and confused.

"You have customers waiting," Gideon reminded her, without turning around.

Now the man had eyes on the back of his head as well as cooking skills?

Again...*what the hell?*

Shaking her head, she returned to the window and the ever-growing line outside. For the next couple hours, the three of them worked like a well-oiled machine. Shay still couldn't quite grasp that Gideon Knight was there in the cramped quarters of a food truck, cooking Thai entrées like a professional.

She tried to imagine Trevor jumping in and helping out and couldn't. The image refused to solidify, because her brother would never have done it. Not many men of her acquaintance would've bothered getting their hands dirty. But then again, two hours ago she wouldn't have been able to picture Gideon getting his hands dirty, either. And especially not for her.

As Bridgette closed the serving window and hung the Closed sign, questions crowded into Shay's head. But before she could ask them, he turned, tugging down his sleeves and rebuttoning the cuffs.

"I'll be by to pick you up at seven tonight for a dinner party. This time, be there and ready," Gideon ordered, thrusting his arms into his jacket, then his coat, his tone warning her not to argue. And for once, she heeded it. "And don't keep me waiting."

With a brisk nod at Bridgette, he stalked out the door, leaving a weighty silence behind.

Bridgette was the first to break it.

"What in the hell just happened?" she yelled, voicing the same question that had been plaguing Shay since Gideon's sudden appearance.

And her answer was the same.

Damned if she knew.

* * *

Hours later, Shay stood in the foyer and stared at the front door as the ring of the doorbell echoed through her house.

Seven o'clock. Right on the dot.

Her pulse raced, and the roar of it filled her head, deafening her. Nerves. They waged war inside her, turning her belly into a churned-up battlefield. Any sane woman would be anxious about entering a charade and perpetrating a fraud on everyone she knew and cared about.

But she would be lying to herself if she attributed the lion's share of the nerves to their arrangement. No, that honor belonged to the man himself.

Who was Gideon Knight?

The attentive, protective and devastatingly sensual stranger from the night of the blackout? The aloof billionaire and brilliant CEO of a global tech company? The ruthless, revenge-driven ex-fiancé? The man who barged into a food truck, rolled up his sleeves and selflessly helped serve the Chicago masses?

Which one was real? And why did they all fascinate her?

Exhaling a breath, she rubbed her damp palms down her thighs. No fascination. Or curiosity. Both were hazardous and would only lead to a slippery, dangerous slope. One where she could convince herself that the tender, generous man was the true one, and the one who held her brother's future over her head was the aberration.

What had been one of her mother's favorite sayings? "When someone shows you who they are, believe them." Well, Gideon had shown her he would go to any lengths, no matter how merciless, to achieve what he wanted. Even if it meant using and hurting other people in the process. She needed to believe this truth.

And accept it.

The doorbell rang again, and it unglued her feet, propelling her forward. She unlocked and opened the door, revealing her date for the evening. No, correction—the man she was madly in love with for the next six months.

Gideon stared down at her, his black eyes slowly traversing the curls and waves she'd opted for tonight, down the black cocktail dress with its sheer side cutouts and sleeves, to the stilettos that added four inches to her height. When his eyes met hers again, she barely caught herself before taking a step back from the heat there. It practically seared her skin.

Hazardous. Dangerous. She silently chanted the warnings to herself like a mantra.

He would set fire to her life and leave her covered in ashes.

"Seven o'clock," she rasped, before clearing her throat of the arousal thickening it. "Just as you requested."

"You're beautiful."

Struck speechless, she could only stare at him. His expression hadn't changed from the cool, distant mask, but those eyes, and now his voice... If his gaze made her tremble, the low, sensual throb in that dark velvet voice had her squeezing her thighs against the ache deep inside her.

"Where's your coat?" he asked, glancing past her into the house.

"I have it."

Get it together, she silently ordered herself as she briefly returned inside to grab her coat off the stand.

"Here. Let me." He stepped inside the foyer and took the cape from her, holding it up while she slipped into it.

Fastening it, she turned back to him, and her voice did another vanishing act when he offered her a crooked elbow. Her breathing shallow, she hesitated, then slid her arm through his and let him guide her out of the house and to his waiting Town Car. A driver stood at the rear door, but Gideon waved him away and opened the door for her himself.

God, she was too old for Cinderella-like fairy tales. If she'd ever had stars in her eyes, they'd been dimmed a long time ago. But here, sitting with Gideon Knight in the back of a car that was more elegant and luxurious than any limousine she'd ridden in, with the heat from his body and his earthy sandalwood scent invading her senses, she could almost understand why Cinderella had lost a beautiful shoe over a man.

"I didn't have a chance to tell you earlier, but… thank you. For stepping in and helping Bridgette this afternoon." She glanced at his sharply hewn profile. "How do you know how to cook? I wouldn't have expected it of…a man like you."

He turned to her, and even in the shadowed interior, his dark eyes gleamed. Dim light from the streetlamps passed over his face, highlighting then hiding his toohandsome features. She fought the urge to stroke her fingertips over those planes and angles, over the full curves of his mouth. Free those thick, silken strands and tangle her fingers in them…

"A man like me?" he repeated, the sardonic note relaying that he understood exactly what she meant. "I hate to tarnish your image of me, Shay, but my beginnings aren't as rarefied as yours and your brother's. My grandparents immigrated from China with nothing more than they could carry, and both of my parents worked barely above minimum-wage jobs when I was a kid. When my father died, Mom often worked two jobs to provide for us. And as soon as I was old enough, I took any kind of employment I could to help her. One of those happened to be as a short-order cook. If you ever need your yard landscaped or your gutters cleaned, I can do those, too."

Shame sidled through her in a slick, oily glide. She'd unknowingly spoken from a lofty place of privilege, but her ignorance didn't excuse it. True, she didn't subscribe to the idle lives some of those in high society did—she believed in working hard and making a difference in the world—but she couldn't deny that she didn't know what it was to go without. To go to bed exhausted from menial labor or worried about how the next bill would be paid.

Gideon's mother, and even Gideon, obviously did.

"I'm sorry," she murmured. "I spoke out of turn." She paused, debated whether to say anything else, but ended up whispering, "Your mother must be proud of you."

He studied her for several silent, heavy moments. "She is. But then again, she would've been proud of me if I'd decided to remain a short-order cook in a fast-food restaurant."

Shay digested that, turned it over and analyzed it again. Could she say the same for her parents? *No.* Her father would've easily disowned her. And as much as Shay adored her mother, Leida Neal wouldn't have been proud of or happy for her daughter if she had been anything less than what her name demanded— respectable, wealthy, connected and married to a man who fit those same qualifications.

The certainty in that knowledge saddened her. Did Gideon realize how fortunate he was?

"She sounds lovely," Shay said, ready to drop the unsettling subject. But then, because her mouth apparently had no allegiance to her, she blurted out, "I'm sorry about your father."

Another heartbeat of weighty silence.

"It was a long time ago."

"My mother died fourteen years ago. And I still miss her every day," she admitted softly.

Slowly, he nodded. "I remember," he finally said, surprising her. "Your brother and I went to high school together, and later attended the same college. But I recall when your mother died. The principal came for him in the middle of class and took him out."

"I didn't know you and Trevor went to school together." Shock whistled through her. "He never mentioned knowing you." Not that he mentioned Gideon at all unless it regarded acquiring his tech company.

"FAST FIVE" READER SURVEY

Your participation entitles you to:
✳ **4 Thank-You Gifts Worth Over $20!**

Complete the survey in minutes.

Get **2 FREE** Books

See inside for details.

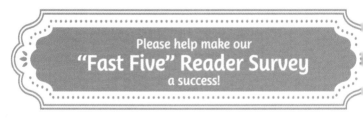

Please help make our
"Fast Five" Reader Survey
a success!

Dear Reader,

Since you are a lover of our books, your opinions are important to us... and so is your time.

That's why we made sure your **"FAST FIVE" READER SURVEY** can be completed in just a few minutes. Your answers to the five questions will help us remain at the forefront of women's fiction.

And, as a thank-you for participating, we'd like to send you **4 FREE THANK-YOU GIFTS!**

Enjoy your gifts with our appreciation,

Pam Powers

To get your
4 FREE THANK-YOU GIFTS:

✳ Quickly complete the "Fast Five" Reader Survey
and return the insert.

▼ DETACH AND MAIL CARD TODAY! ▼

"FAST FIVE" READER SURVEY

#	Question		
1	Do you sometimes read a book a second or third time?	○ Yes	○ No
2	Do you often choose reading over other forms of entertainment such as television?	○ Yes	○ No
3	When you were a child, did someone regularly read aloud to you?	○ Yes	○ No
4	Do you sometimes take a book with you when you travel outside the home?	○ Yes	○ No
5	In addition to books, do you regularly read newspapers and magazines?	○ Yes	○ No

YES! I have completed the above Reader Survey. Please send me my 4 FREE GIFTS (gifts worth over $20 retail). I understand that I am under no obligation to buy anything, as explained on the back of this card.

225/326 HDL GNQC

FIRST NAME	LAST NAME

ADDRESS

APT.#	CITY

STATE/PROV.	ZIP/POSTAL CODE

READER SERVICE—Here's how it works:

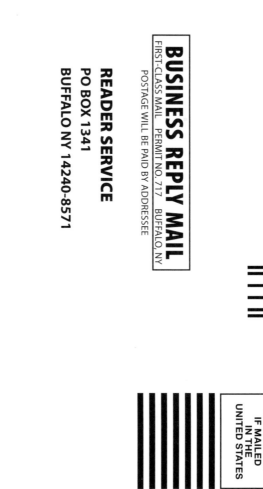

BUSINESS REPLY MAIL

FIRST-CLASS MAIL   PERMIT NO. 717   BUFFALO, NY

POSTAGE WILL BE PAID BY ADDRESSEE

READER SERVICE

PO BOX 1341

BUFFALO NY 14240-8571

NO POSTAGE
NECESSARY
IF MAILED
IN THE
UNITED STATES

If offer card is missing write to: Reader Service, P.O. Box 1341, Buffalo, NY 14240-8531 or visit www.ReaderService.com

Or more recently, not unless a blue streak of unflattering adjectives followed his name.

His sensual mouth curved into a hard, faintly cruel smile. "Your brother and I have a long history. He was decent until that day. I was a scholarship student at an elite, private prep school. That already made me a target for most students there. But your brother wasn't one of them. Until after your mother died. Then he became one of the worst. That he and I were often head-to-head competitors in academics and athletics didn't help matters. Neither did the fact that I didn't take his or any of the other assholes' shit."

"He changed after Mother passed," Shay murmured, the dagger of pain stabbing her chest all too familiar when she thought about the boy who'd become a hardened man. "She was the...buffer between him and my father. My dad..." Shay shook her head, turning to stare at the passing scenery outside the car window, but seeing Lincoln Neal's disapproving, stern frown that was often directed at his children. But more so at his first-born child. "He was demanding, exacting and nearly impossible to please. And Trevor desperately wanted to please him. Which became impossible after our father died. Yet, even now..." Again she trailed off, feeling as if she betrayed her brother by revealing even that much.

"That doesn't excuse his behavior," Gideon replied, ice coating his voice.

"No," she agreed, more to herself than him. "But no one is created in a bubble. And no one is all bad or all good. Sometimes it helps to understand why people behave the way they do. And it helps us give them compassion and mercy."

Strong, firm fingers gripped her chin and turned her to face him. Gideon's touch reverberated through her, echoing in the taut tips of her breasts, low in her belly, and in the pulsing flesh between her thighs. He'd clutched her like this the night of the blackout, holding her in place, so he could watch her as she came. Now, like then, she couldn't tear her gaze away from his. Like then, her lips parted, but now, she swallowed down the whimper that clawed at the back of her throat.

"Your brother doesn't deserve compassion or mercy, Shay. So don't try to convince me differently with sad stories of his childhood." He swept the pad of his thumb over her bottom lip, and this time she lost the battle and released that small sound of need. His eyes narrowed on her mouth, then after several moments, lifted to meet hers. "Why does it feel like I've—" He frowned, but didn't remove his hand.

"Why does it feel like you've what?" she breathed, dread filtering into the desire. He'd heard her plead for him, for his touch, many times during the night they'd spent together. Had the sound she'd released just now triggered his memory?

God, in hindsight, she should've been up front with him about her identity from the beginning. If she came clean now, he would only see her as a liar.

Maybe because you're lying by omission?

Shame crept in, mingling with the dread. She hated deception of any kind, and this didn't sit well with her. At all. But self-preservation trumped her conscience at this point. Her reasons for initially remaining quiet still stood. She didn't trust Gideon. Didn't know what he would do with the information that Shay Neal had masqueraded as waitstaff at one of the biggest social events of the year and then slept with him under false pretenses. Would he use it as another source of ammo in this war he waged with her brother, leaving her reputation and her company as casualties?

Possibly.

No, she couldn't afford to find out.

"Nothing." He dropped his hand from her face, his customary impassive expression falling firmly back in place. Turning from her, he picked up a small, rectangular box from the seat beside him. "Here. I have something for you."

She glanced down at the gift, then back up at him. After several moments, she returned her attention to the box and, with slightly trembling fingers, removed the lid. And gasped.

Delicate ruby-and-gold bangles nestled on black velvet. Tiny diamonds rimmed the bracelets, making the jewelry glitter in the dark.

They were beautiful. Just…beautiful.

"There're eight of them," he said, picking up the bangles when she didn't make a move toward them. "In Chinese culture, eight is a lucky number. Red is also lucky."

Gently grasping her hand, he slid the jewelry onto her wrist.

"Thank you," she whispered. In the past, she'd received earrings, necklaces and rings from men who hoped to win her over—or rather win over the Neal heiress. But none of them had been bought with thought or meaning. None of them had been for *her*, Shay. Whether he'd intended it or not, Gideon had given her a piece of himself, of his heritage. And for that alone, she'd accept. "They're gorgeous."

"You're welcome," he murmured, his fingers brushing over the tender skin on the inside of her wrist before withdrawing. For a moment, she caught a flicker of emotion in his eyes before he shut her out once again.

She felt the echo deep inside her.

And for some inexplicable reason—a reason she refused to explore—it hurt.

A charade, she reminded herself. They were both playing their parts, and gifts to his fake girlfriend were part of those roles.

As long as she kept that truth forefront in her mind, she wouldn't get caught up in the beautiful enigma that was Gideon Knight.

Eleven

"I feel like a zoo animal in a cage," Shay muttered, lifting a glass of white wine to her lips. "They could at least be subtler about the staring."

Gideon arched an eyebrow, scanning the large formal living room. Several pairs of eyes met, then slid away from his, caught ogling the newest couple in their midst. Satisfaction whispered through him. He'd accepted this particular dinner party invitation because of who would be in attendance. Not just business associates, but members of the social circle Shay was intricately a part of. Talk of their appearance together would rush through Chicago's society elite like a brush fire.

"They're wondering why you're with the beast," he said.

"Probably."

He snorted at her quick agreement, earning a dazzling smile from her. He had to hand it to her—Shay was a brilliant actress. As soon as they'd crossed the threshold into Janet and Donald's mansion, she'd immediately charmed his client and her husband. And though he knew the truth behind their arrangement, even he could almost believe Shay was smitten with him. Small, but intimate touches to his arm and chest. Gentle teasing. Special smiles. Yes, she deserved an award for her performance.

And as their hosts approached them, and she slid her arm through his, her soft breast pressing into side, he ordered his dick to stand down for about the fifty-fifth time...in two hours.

If he was a better man, he would insert some distance between them, not enjoy the sensual lure of her scent. Or savor each time he settled a palm at the small of her back—a back covered only by the same sheer material that "covered" her shoulders and arms. She was sex and class in this dress that skimmed every delicious curve.

Damn if the heat from her didn't seep into his palm and ignite every greedy need to stroke her skin, sift his fingers through the thick, dark strands of her hair... claim her saint-and-sinner body for his own.

The only woman to have stirred this unprecedented reaction in him had been Camille. It unsettled him. The mysterious waitress was no longer in his life. But Shay... Everything about her tested his control, his reason, his plans.

How he kept touching her when every rule of logic demanded he keep all displays of affection public to cement the facade of a happy, in-love couple. How she challenged him with those flashes of temper when no one except his best friend and business partner dared. How she surprised him with things like working in a food truck. How he couldn't jettison the sense that there was something familiar about her...

And then there was his jewelry on her wrist. The gold and rubies gleamed against her skin like sunlight and fire. And that fierce surge of possessiveness that had blindsided him in the car swelled within him again. He braced himself against it.

This wasn't the first time he'd bought a woman jewelry. Hell, the amount he'd bought Madison could have filled a store and still left enough diamonds to pay for a small city. He'd gone into the store this time intending to purchase a necklace or earrings, something that screamed wealth. But none of the pieces had felt...right. So he'd left, and instead had driven to a smaller jeweler. One where he'd bought his grandmother's birthday gift. And the bangles had been there, waiting. He hadn't intended to purchase something so personal to him, so...intimate, for what should've been just a flashy statement of ownership, with the sole purpose of making others take note. But he had. And unlike almost everything in his life, he didn't analyze it, instead going on impulse.

Because in that moment, as he'd handed his credit card over the counter, his need to see Shay wearing the pieces he'd personally chosen far outweighed caution.

And that need hadn't abated.

As he slid his hand up her spine and cupped the nape of her neck, the need deepened, sharpened.

"I should be annoyed with both of you," Janet Creighton said, her smile erasing the reproach from her words. Leaning forward, she dropped her voice to a conspiratorial whisper. "But the two of you outing yourselves as a couple tonight has made my little dinner party the social event of the season."

Shay smiled, glancing up at Gideon, and the warmth reflected in the gold-and-green depths of her eyes had his breath stumbling in his throat. "I told Gideon he should at least give you some warning of who his plus one would be, but..." She tipped her head to the side and murmured, "The rumors are true about that stubborn nature of his."

"I find myself giving in to you way too often, though. My reputation might not survive it," he replied, squeezing her neck and bringing her closer, brushing his lips over the side of her head.

Her fingernails bit into his arm, and he barely managed to fight back a groan. The tiny prick of pain echoed lower in his body, and he locked his jaw against asking her to do it again. But harder.

"You shouldn't let me know I'm a weakness," she teased, but only he caught the undercurrent of faint sarcasm. "I might be tempted to take advantage."

"I might be tempted to let you," he rejoined softly.

Silence thrummed between them, taut and tension-filled. Their gazes clashed, tangled, locked. The pretense seemed all too real. As did the desire that flared inside him, the excitement that flashed through him, as bright and hot as a bolt of lightning. What would she do if he lowered his head and took her soft mouth? Would she jerk away from him? Or would she use their act as an excuse to surrender, to let him taste her?

"Well, damn." Janet's awed, but amused whisper infiltrated the haze of arousal that had clouded him and his judgment. *Damn it,* he silently swore, returning his attention to his client. This was a facade, an act. One he'd set in motion. He couldn't afford to forget that. "Honey, I need you to take notes."

Beside Janet, her husband snorted lightly. "We've been married thirty-two years. My hand is cramped."

Shay's laughter drew more gazes in their direction, and Gideon smiled, both at the other couple and the pure delight in Shay's amusement.

"Dinner is almost ready," Janet said, shaking her head and throwing Donald a mock-irritated glance. "Let's go, you."

"That went well," Shay murmured, as soon as they were out of earshot. She slowly released his arm. "You can let go of me now."

Instead of obeying, he turned into her body, his hold on her drawing her closer until her breasts brushed his chest. He caught her sharp gasp, felt the puff against the base of his throat. Tiny flickers danced under his skin at that spot.

She stiffened, and he softly tsked, lowering his voice so it carried only as far as her ears. "You're supposed to enjoy my touch, Shay. Want more of it. But definitely not shy away from it." When she lifted her hands and settled them at his waist under his jacket, her fingernails digging into his skin through his shirt, he didn't hold back his low rumble of hunger. "I think you're intending to punish me, moonbeam," he growled above her mouth, pinching her chin with his free hand and tilting her head back. "But I don't mind a bit of pain with my pleasure. Would you sink those claws in deeper if I asked nicely?"

He expected her to wrench away from him; his muscles tightened in anticipation of controlling the reaction he purposefully coaxed from her.

But she sank her nails harder into his flesh, and the stings were a precursor of how she would scratch and grip him if they were stretched out on his bed. He tried to swallow his groan, but some sound escaped against his will. And the molten gold in her eyes almost eclipsed the brown and green.

She'd played him. Turned the tables so completely he ground his teeth together, imprisoning the words that would reveal she'd knocked him on his ass. Those words being *more, harder, please...*

"Gideon," she whispered.

"Well, don't you two look cozy," a new, all-too-familiar and despised voice drawled from behind them.

Gideon released Shay, shifting to her side and slipping an arm around her waist. He faced Madison and Julian Reus, careful to compose his features so they betrayed none of the disgust and hatred that burned in his chest for her, or the disdain he harbored for her father.

Underneath those emotions, satisfaction hummed

through his veins. *Good.* He'd been waiting for their arrival. He'd expected Trevor to be with them, but since he wasn't glued to Madison's side, the other man must not be in attendance. That was a disappointment, but Gideon's cheating ex and her equally deceptive father were good enough.

He switched his attention to Madison. It stunned him that he'd once missed the avaricious, calculating gleam in her brown eyes. Given her long dark hair, sensuous features and curvaceous body, he couldn't deny her beauty, but it was hard, like a lacquer that distracted from the coldness beneath.

Love had truly been blind. No. It'd made him dumb and deaf, too.

"I must admit, when we heard the rumors of you being here with Gideon, Shay, we didn't believe it at first," Julian said, his tone as amicable as any good politician's. But his eyes blazed, yelling the things one would never want heard on an open lapel mic. "Your brother didn't mention you were attending tonight. Or that you were…" he paused deliberately "…seeing someone new. I'm sure he'll be interested to discover this turn of events."

If the senator had expected Shay to quail under his not-so-subtle condemnation, he'd sadly underestimated her. "Trevor is a wonderful brother, but he's just that— my brother. And I don't require his approval for who I choose to spend time with. Just as he didn't ask for mine with Madison." Shay smiled, and it could've cut glass. "Although I would've gladly offered it."

Julian blinked, his mouth hardening at the corners.

"Your brother and I have much in common. We both admire honesty—and loyalty."

"You don't really want to go there, do you, Julian?" Gideon interjected, arching an eyebrow. He forced his voice to remain even, bored, but injected a thread of steel through it. He'd be damned if he'd let the man intimidate Shay or belittle her with his condescending bullshit. Especially not in front of him. "I'd be willing to discuss both with you. At length."

"Let's go, Daddy." Madison chuckled, the sound strained, her lovely features tight. Like her father's, her gaze ordered Gideon to do unnatural things with his own anatomy. "There are more people we need to speak with."

Shay waited until her soon-to-be sister-in-law and her father were out of earshot, then sighed. "God. This evening just became infinitely longer."

"I beg to disagree." He settled a hand on the small of her back again, guiding her forward. "The fun has just begun."

Shay breathed deeply as she washed her hands in the Creightons' bathroom. This moment alone, without the narrow-eyed glares from both Madison and the senator, or the microscopic attention of the other guests, was a mercy.

She hated being the subject of all that speculation. They'd reminded her of vultures, waiting to see who'd get their pick of carrion. Gideon seemed unfazed. But all those sidelong, greedy glances and not-so-quiet whispers… They'd crawled over her like ants attacking a picnic. By the time dinner concluded, she'd nearly raced to the bathroom. To be free. If only for a few moments.

"Can't stay in here forever," she said to her reflection.

That was the first sign of losing it, right? Talking to oneself. She smiled, shaking her head as she headed toward the restroom door. Her mother used to do the same, mumble to herself as she puttered around the kitchen when Dad wasn't there to catch her. God, Shay missed her. Missed her hugs, her quiet assurances, her confidence in Shay.

Well, one thing Leida Neal would've reprimanded her about was hiding like a coward in the bathroom during a dinner party. Snorting lightly, Shay exited the powder room...and nearly collided with Madison.

Damn.

"Hi, Madison." She greeted her brother's fiancée with a smile. "I'm sorry if you had to wait. The bathroom's all yours."

She shifted to the side, prepared to walk around the other woman, but the futile hope of avoiding a confrontation died a quick death when Madison stepped to the side as well, blocking Shay's escape. Madison smiled in turn, but it didn't reach her chilly brown eyes.

"No hurry, Shay. I was hoping to catch you alone for a few moments," she purred. "We have so much to catch up on, seeing as we apparently have more in common than I thought."

"I'm assuming you're referring to Gideon," Shay said, resigning herself to this conversation. It wasn't one she could've circumvented, but she hadn't anticipated having it outside of the guest restroom.

"You're a cool one, aren't you, Shay?" Madison asked, slowly shaking her head. "The other night you never mentioned you knew him. And when I told you about our past, you pretended to be dumb. It seems I underestimated you. I won't repeat the mistake."

Anger flickered to life, crackling like dry wood set ablaze. "I didn't pretend to be dumb, as you put it. Discussing my private life while you were at the table with my brother, your fiancé, didn't strike me as appropriate. And like I told your father, I don't need approval for my relationships," she said, working to keep the bite of rising irritation from her tone. After all, this was her future sister-in-law. Even if more and more she was beginning to question the wisdom of Trevor's choice. "Now, if I'd known you were attending this dinner party, I would've informed you so you weren't taken by surprise. But I wasn't aware."

Several silent moments passed, and a fury-filled tension thickened between them.

"Your brother always brags about how smart you are." Madison tsked softly. "Shay earned this degree. Shay graduated with honors from this program. So intelligent. And yet, when it comes to men, you're so naive." Her expression softened with a sympathy that was as false as her lashes. "What are the odds that *my ex* would turn around and fall for *my new fiancé's sister*? A little too coincidental, don't you think?" She chuckled, the sound taunting. "It's almost pathetic in its transparency. He's using you, Shay. Gideon still wants me, and you're caught up in his little plan to make me jealous."

Pain, serrated and ugly, slashed at her, the truth of Madison's words the razor-sharp knife. Why did it hurt? She'd gone into this charade knowing the reason behind it. Gideon hadn't tried to deny it. But reason had no place when humiliation and pain pumped out of her with every heartbeat.

Forcing her lips to move and her arm to lift, she waved away Madison's barb-tipped claims as if they were petty annoyances. "I don't see how any of this is your business, Madison. What is between Gideon and me is just that. *Between us*. Now if you'll excuse me..."

She moved forward again. If Madison chose to get in the way, this time she'd find her ass meeting the floor. Thankfully, Madison didn't try to block her, and Shay headed toward the dining room with a smothered sigh of relief.

"Ask him who broke it off with whom. He hasn't let go of me. If I wanted him back, Shay, he would be mine."

Madison's parting shot struck true. By sheer force of will, Shay kept walking.

But it was with a limp.

Twelve

"You ambushed me. Again."

Gideon turned from his silent—okay, brooding—study of the scenery passing by the car window to look at Shay. She'd been quiet since they'd left the Creightons' mansion ten minutes earlier. No, she'd been distant since returning to the dining room after dinner.

And Madison had followed a couple minutes behind her, wearing a sly grin. Personal experience had taught him his ex could be a malicious bitch. Had she said something to Shay? Had Madison hurt her? A wave of protectiveness had surged inside him, and he'd just managed to check the impulse to drag Shay onto his lap and demand answers. To ease the tension that had strung her shoulders tight. To assure her that if Madison had sharpened that dagger she called a tongue against Shay, he would fix it.

Instead, he'd remained sitting beside her at the table, continuing the charade until they could politely leave.

Disgust ate at him like a caustic acid. Disgust with himself. He'd led her into the lion's den and hadn't shielded her.

Every war has casualties.

He mentally repeated the reminder like a mantra. He'd been aware when he'd included Shay as part of his plans that she might be wounded, but the end justified the means. He intentionally conjured an image of his sister lying on that hospital bed, black hair limp, skin pale as she stared listlessly out the window. Oh yes. The end justified the means. *Olivia*—her suffering, her brokenness, her loss—justified it.

"Am I supposed to know what that cryptic comment means, Shay?" he asked. "Because I can assure you, I don't."

She didn't flinch from his flat, indifferent tone or the dismissal in his question. "You knew Madison and the senator would be there tonight."

Gideon stared at her, not even debating whether to give her the truth or not. "Of course I did. Janet and Donald are business associates of Julian's."

"You didn't think to warn me?" She shook her head. "What if Trevor had been there?"

"And?" he asked, anger igniting inside him. "I hoped he would be. But it doesn't matter. Maybe him hearing about his sister dating his enemy from his future father-in-law or his fiancée might work out better than I intended."

"Do you care that your schemes and plans are hurting people?" she whispered.

The disappointment in her voice, as if he'd somehow let her down, raked over his skin. Burrowed beneath it.

He hated it.

Dipping his head, he leaned closer until only inches separated them. So close her breath ghosted over his lips. "Your brother?" He paused. "No."

"All this for her," she breathed, her gold-and-green eyes roaming his face. Summer on the verge of autumn. That's what they reminded him of. Shaking his head as if he could physically rid himself of the sentimental thought, he leaned away from her, turning back to the window. "Madison was right."

He stiffened, his suspicions confirmed.

Slowly, he straightened and shifted on the seat, meeting her gaze again.

"What did she say to you?" he growled.

"Nothing I didn't already know," she replied, her full bottom lip trembling before she seemed to catch the betraying sign. Her teeth sank into the sensual curve.

"What did she say to you, Shay?" he repeated, grounding out the question between clenched teeth.

"That you were using me to get back at her and Trevor. That she could have you back if she wanted. She…" Shay paused, and something flickered in her eyes. "She told me to ask you who broke up with whom. From that, I'm assuming she left you."

He didn't answer. Couldn't.

What did it matter if Shay knew the dirty details? Of how he'd walked in on her brother in Madison's bed. How the woman he'd believed he would spend the rest of his life with had told him she'd upgraded with Trevor.

None of it mattered now. Yet he couldn't shove the words past his throat.

Shay shook her head, chuckling softly. Except the sound contained no humor. "So is that your master plan? Was the file on my brother your way of ensuring I cooperated while you plotted to steal back your ex? That would show Trevor who the better man was, right? Teach him—"

"You don't know what you're talking about."

"That's another thing Madison accused me of being. Dumb. But I'm not. You're fighting over her like she's some ball you lost on the playground. And in the end, I'll look like the idiot she called me. But that doesn't matter to you, does it? Not as long as you win."

Her accusation struck too close to the doubts that had pricked at his conscience only moments before. That only stirred his anger.

He didn't give a damn if she knew the truth.

"Win?" He arched an eyebrow, not bothering to prevent his sneer. "Win what, exactly? A relationship based on lies and greed? A woman who would jump to the next dick as long as he was willing to pay handsomely for the privilege? Tell me, Shay, doesn't that sound like a terrible grand prize?"

She gaped at him, no doubt stunned by the ferocity of his reply. "What do you mean?" she asked, her gaze roaming his face, as if searching for the truth. As if she actually wanted the truth. "Do you mean she—"

"Cheated on me? Oh yes." He nodded, and the smile on his mouth felt savage. "We'd been together a year and a half, engaged to be married. Gorgeous, fun, witty, exciting—I didn't care who her father was or about her family name. All I wanted was her. And all she wanted was what I could give her. At least, until she found someone else who could give her more. Care to guess who that someone was?"

Her lips formed her brother's name, but no sound came out.

"Yes, Trevor. I came home early from a business trip and stopped by her place. I had the key, so I went in and found them together. In the bed I'd just made love to her in two days earlier. It hadn't been the first time they'd been together. The next day, when giving me back my ring, Madison informed me that it'd been going on for some time—six months. According to her, I might be rich, but Trevor had prestige, connections and a family name. She'd upgraded."

Shay's chin jerked up as if he'd delivered a verbal punch to her jaw. Sorrow flashed in her eyes, and for a second, he resented her for it. He didn't want her pity; he wanted her to understand the kind of bastard she called brother.

"Your brother did it on purpose, Shay," he pressed.

Just as he'd used Gideon's sister to get to him. "He went after Madison because she was my fiancée, and faithless bitch that she is, she had no problem sleeping with a man she knew I hated. She not only betrayed me with her body, but with her loyalty, her heart. So I don't need to prove to Trevor who the better man is. Because, Shay, your brother isn't a real one."

"Gideon," she whispered.

"No." He slashed a hand down between them, done with the topic. Done with laying out his stupidity before her. "And to address the second part of that statement, you're not dumb. Far from it. But you are blind." He narrowed his eyes on her. "Why are you so quick to believe the manipulative claims of a jealous woman?"

She blinked. "What do you mean?" She frowned. "Madison's not—"

"Jealous," he interrupted again. "Why is that so hard to accept?" He didn't wait for her to answer, but continued. "And this doesn't have anything to do with me. You're everything she wants to be. Respected. Admired not just for your beauty but for who you are—successful, brilliant, esteemed. She, like me, like Julian, watched as you charmed everyone around you tonight, and as they damn near competed to have a moment of your time. And that has nothing to do with your last name. That's all you. I'm the toy in this scenario, moonbeam," he murmured. The thought of being her plaything roughened his voice, tightened his gut. "And she wants me only because you—a woman she could never be—has me."

If he hadn't been watching her so closely, he

might've missed her flinch before she controlled it. "Why are you calling me that?" she rasped.

"The other women there tonight… They were like the sun—bright, obvious. Trying so hard to be noticed. But you, Shay, you don't have to try to grab someone's attention. Like the moon, you're distant, cool and beautiful. Men can't help but notice you. Be drawn to you, ready to beg for some of your light rather than be lost and alone in the dark."

Only the harsh grating of their breaths filled the back of the car. Part of him demanded he rescind those too-revealing words. But the other part—the greedy, desperate part—refused to, instead waiting to see what she would do with them.

"What game are you playing now, Gideon?" she whispered, her eyes wide…vulnerable. "I don't know how to play this one."

"Then set the rules," he said, just as softly. Unable not to touch her any longer, he cupped her deceptively delicate jaw, stroked the pad of his thumb over the elegant jut of her cheekbone. "Set the rules, and I'll follow them."

It was a dangerous allowance. In this "relationship" the balance of power couldn't shift; he couldn't hand her a weapon to use against him. Not when revenge for his sister's pain, his family's torment hung in the balance. But that knowledge didn't stop him from shifting closer to her, from tipping her head back and brushing a caress over her parted lips. From staring down into those beautiful eyes and letting her see the desire that hurtled through his veins.

"Just one. Make…" She paused, briefly closed her eyes, but then her lashes lifted. "Make me forget."

"Forget what, moonbeam?"

The answer was already yes. He'd surrender anything to her if she'd permit him to continue touching her.

But that same hunger to brand her vied with the need to conquer what haunted her. He'd never considered himself some knight facing dragons, not for anyone, but for Shay, he'd forgo the armor and charge into the fire.

One hand rose to his wrist, the slender fingers wrapping around and hanging on to him. The other slipped inside his jacket and settled on his chest before sliding up to his neck, her thumb resting on his pulse.

"Forget that you're trying to destroy my brother, my world," she whispered. "Forget that you're going to break me. And I'm going to let you."

A vise gripped his chest and tightened until the barest of breaths passed through his lungs. If he was a good man, he would release her, promise not to touch her again. Walk away from this whole plan that already ensnared her like barbed wire. She was right; he would probably end up hurting her, and if he had a conscience, he would warn her to protect herself from him.

But he'd never claimed to be good.

Still, he could do what she asked. He could make her forget.

"Kiss me," he ordered in a low rumble. "Take what you want—what you need from me. And, moonbeam?"

He lowered his head, pushing his thumb past the seam of her lips and into her mouth. Moist heat bathed the tip. "Don't be gentle," he growled.

She studied him, and as he watched her in turn, desire eclipsed the vulnerability that lingered in her gaze. He felt her teeth first, and the tiny sting arrowed straight to his lower body.

"Don't be gentle," he repeated, harder.

Her eyes still on him, she moved the hand on his neck so her fingers encircled the front. She squeezed just as her lips closed around his thumb, and she bit him.

"Fuck," he groaned, the sting arcing through him like a sizzling bolt of electricity. "Baby." Her gaze darted to the side, toward the front of the car and his driver. "The divide is soundproof," he assured her, pulling his thumb free and rubbing the dampness over her bottom lip. Before repaying her with a nip of his own.

Another moan clawed free of him. Damn, he'd been aching—literally *aching*—to get his mouth on her. To taste her. Reaching for the console in front of the seat, he lifted the hood and hit a button, and another panel, this one smoke-tinted, slid across, concealing them.

"Are you good?" he asked. His dick throbbed, and he gritted his teeth.

He could wait until they reached their destination, but fuck if he *or* his dick wanted to. He needed to be inside her. From the moment he'd sat down across from her in that restaurant, he'd craved this. No, damn that. Longer. From the second he'd opened his private investigator's file and laid eyes on her picture. Even as he'd spun his plans of revenge, he'd envisioned those hazel eyes gleaming with the arousal he'd stirred. Pictured her sweet body bowing and twisting for him. Wondered if she would take him slow and easy, or hard and wild. God, he'd almost driven himself insane wondering that.

She nodded, but he shook his head. "Tell me, moonbeam. You good?"

"Yes," she breathed, giving his neck one last squeeze. She removed her hand, replacing it with her mouth, trailing a path up his throat, over his chin until she hovered over his lips. "I've set the rules," she reminded him, kneeling on the seat so she rose over him. "Now follow them like you promised."

She crushed her mouth to his.

The kiss wasn't patient, wasn't tentative. Her tongue thrust forward, parried with his, tangling and dueling. She took him as if she knew exactly what he liked, what he needed. It was…familiar. Something—a thought, a warning, maybe—tickled the back of his skull, but as she sucked on his tongue, drawing on him as if he were everything she needed to survive, that inkling winked out. Nothing mattered but the intoxicating, addictive taste of her. And in that instant, the question that had plagued him since he first gazed on her picture was answered: Shay would be hard and wild in bed. Or in the back of a Town Car.

"I want to…" She didn't finish her request, but reached behind him, removing the band holding back his hair.

The strands loosened, and her heavy sigh differed from the ones she'd been emitting during their kiss. This one? It matched the delight that softened her beautiful features as she drew his hair forward and up to her face. Tangling her fingers in the strands, she tugged on them, and the prickle across his scalp tripped down his spine, crackled at the base. He clutched her hips, digging his fingertips into the soft flesh.

"Beautiful," she whispered.

Only one other woman had ever called him that, and with that same note of awe coating the compliment. It'd shaken him then, and it did now. Once more that niggling sense of…something…teased him. But he shoved it away. Now, with his hands on Shay, with her storm-whipped rain and fresh roses scent embracing him, there wasn't room for thoughts of another woman. Especially one that was a ghost. Shay was sensual, golden-bronze flesh-and-bone. She was hot, pounding blood coursing through him. She was his insanity, his hunger brought to vivid life.

She was *here*.

For him.

With a growl, he skated his palms up the sides of her torso, and the zipper of her dress abraded his skin. Desperate to discover if his imagination matched reality, he impatiently tugged it down and wasted no time in pushing the material over her shoulders and down her arms. She obliged him, freeing his hair and joining him in getting rid of the clothing.

"No." The word escaped him before he could trap it.

"No?" she repeated, and he caught the hint of insecurity that crept into her voice. She started to lift her arms toward her torso, but he latched on to her wrists, lowering her arms back down before she could cross them.

"My imagination doesn't match reality. Doesn't even fucking compete." He cupped a breast and hissed at the delicious weight of her flesh filling his palm. Warm, soft, perfect. Reverently, he whisked his thumb over the nipple, watching in fascination as it beaded. No, she wasn't the first woman he'd touched like this, but none had been *her*. He tore his gaze from his hand on her to meet her eyes. "Nothing or no one could fucking compete."

Her lips parted, but no words emerged. Good. He was saying enough for both of them, and he needed to stop that before he took them somewhere they had no place being. Bending his head, he sucked a tip deep, flicking his tongue against her flesh before drawing hard. Shay shuddered, her hands cradling his head, holding him to her with a strength that telegraphed her passion. That and the nails pricking his scalp.

Switching breasts, he treated the other to the same devotion. She writhed against him, as if seeking to get closer. Cooperating, he fisted the hem of her dress and shoved it up her thighs. With a whimper, she straddled him, dropping down and pressing them sex to sex.

He growled around her flesh, suckling harder. And she rewarded his attention with a dirty grind of her hips that had him throwing his head back against the seat, eyes squeezed closed. Her panties and his pants and underwear separated them, but none of those inconsequential details mattered. Not when her hot, wet heat rode him. Not when each drag of her flesh over his cock shredded his control.

"Give me your mouth again," he ordered, in a voice so guttural he barely understood himself.

But she must've translated it, because she gave him what he asked for, her hips still working over him. She didn't stop, and the thrust of her tongue and pull of her lips mimicked each stroke below. Even as she yanked his jacket open and attacked his shirt, damn near ripping buttons loose to get her hands on his bare chest, she didn't lose him.

They groaned into each other when she touched him. Those slender, clever hands swept down his chest, lingering over his tattoos, tracing the ink with almost worshipful strokes.

"How is it possible that you just get more beautiful?" she whispered. He parted his lips to tell her she was the stunning one, not him, but she ripped away his ability to talk by brushing her fingertips over his nipples, rubbing them. His hips bucked into her. Live wires connected from her touch to the tip of his dick. He swelled, throbbing, *hurting*.

"I need to be inside you," he rasped against her mouth. He abandoned her breasts and burrowed his fingers in her hair, gripping it, holding her still so he could stare into those slumberous eyes. "Are you going to let me?"

"Yes," she breathed, trailing a route of fire over his clenched abs to the band of his pants.

"Are you going to take me like this?" he pressed,

thrusting upward so she fully understood what he meant. "Take me like you own me?"

"Yes."

Almost too rough, he released her, reaching into his inner jacket pocket for his wallet. Quickly withdrawing a condom, he tossed the billfold to the floor. Within moments, he had his pants opened, his erection freed. Her swift intake of breath preceded the hot, tight clasp of her fist around him by seconds. His back bowed under the whip of pleasure, and his free hand wrapped around hers, so they pumped his flesh together. For several torturous and blissful moments, they stroked him, pushing closer to an ending that wouldn't include him balls-deep inside her.

"Enough," he muttered, and, removing their hands, tore open the small foil package and slid the protection over him. Above him, she fumbled under her dress, trying to push black lace panties down her hips. "Fuck that," he growled.

Shoving her dress higher until it encircled her waist like a band, he fisted the front of her underwear and jerked it to the side. For a couple seconds, he savored the vision of her bare, glistening sex and the erotic beauty of her silken thigh-high stockings against silkier skin. But then the lure of that feminine flesh proved too enticing, too much.

He slid his finger through the dark cleft, moaning at the wetness coating his skin. The sound dragged from her echoed his, and her head tipped back, shuddering when he circled her, applying minute pressure. Just enough to have her shaking like a leaf, but not enough to catapult her over the edge. That honor belonged to his dick.

Hands grasping his shoulders, she eased down his length, and though the drugging pleasure had his eyes nearly closing to savor the tight, smooth fit of her sex, he kept his attention on her. Because nothing—not the rippling clasp of her body, the quiver of her thighs, the sight of her taking him—could compare with the slight widening and darkening of those beautiful eyes. Those eyes conveyed how much she craved him, needed him.

Those eyes gave him all of her.

And greedy bastard that he was, he wanted it all.

Except for the very fine tremble of his tautly controlled muscles, he held completely still. Allowing her to claim him at her own pace. Even if each interminable second she took to inch down threatened to send him careening into insanity or orgasm—whichever came first. Finally, she sat on his thighs, and he was fully embedded inside her. And still he wouldn't free her from his gaze. Not when, in this moment, surrounded by her sweet flesh, everything clicked into place. He finally knew this gaze.

Knew *her*.

"Fuck me, moonbeam," he whispered. "And don't look away from me."

Sliding her hands over his shoulders and into his hair, she grabbed fistfuls of the strands and glided up his length. Air kissed his tip before she sank onto him again, swallowing him in the firmest, but softest heat. Again. And again. She released him, took him. Eased off him, claimed him.

She rode him, rising and falling over him, driving them both toward the rapidly crumbling edge of release. Her cries mixed with the litany of his own and still she continued to look at him. Letting him see what he did to her. Gifting him with that. Electric pulses zipped up and down his spine, crackling in the balls of his feet. He couldn't hold back much longer. He wasn't going to last.

He loosened a hand from her hair and tucked it between their undulating bodies and slicked it over the top of her sex. Once, twice. A third and a pinch.

She flew apart with a scream, stiffening, her sex gripping him, milking him. Daring him to dive into the abyss with her. Grabbing her hips, he slammed into her, plunging so deep he almost doubted he would ever find his way out of her.

She fucking leveled him.

Her arms closed around his shoulders, cradling him as he bowed his head, groaning out his release into her neck. He inhaled her thick, heady scent as his body calmed and his breathing evened. His senses gradually winked back online after pleasure short-circuited them.

Silence filled the interior of the car. Carefully, he withdrew from her, disposing of the condom and righting their clothes. Shay didn't look at him, paying undue attention to pulling down her dress and settling it around her thighs.

"Are you okay?" he asked, his voice seeming overly loud even to his own ears.

"Yes," she said, still not glancing in his direction.

Camille.

The name shivered on his tongue. He almost said it aloud just to see if she would respond. If her reaction would give her away. But he swallowed the name of the woman who'd haunted his thoughts since the night of the blackout.

The woman who was one and the same as Shay Neal.

It explained the nagging sense of familiarity. The feeling that they'd met before. Sinking into her body had sealed the knowledge for him. How had Shay thought she could continue to fool him once he was deep inside her? How could she believe he would ever forget the too-tight and utterly perfect fit of her?

She'd lied to him. All this time, she'd recognized him—how could she not?—but she'd kept the secret of her identity from him.

Why?

Several reasons entered his mind—embarrassment, protecting her reputation—but one kept blaring in his head, gaining validity.

Had meeting him at the Du Sable City Gala been a setup? Not the blackout, of course, but had she gone to the gala with a plan to meet him? To get close to him? Yes, he'd approached her, but what would've happened if he hadn't? Would she have found a way to get close to him? Found a way to get him to talk to her, to reveal information?

Had Trevor sent her to the gala with that purpose?

Minutes ago, Gideon would've said no. But with the haze of pleasure quickly evaporating and leaving him with a clearer mind, he couldn't know for sure. First and foremost, Shay was a Neal and her loyalty belonged to her brother. Hadn't she been willing to surrender to blackmail and sleep with the enemy— literally, now—to save Trevor? Gideon couldn't see her going so far as to fuck him in that dark break room for her brother. As she'd defiantly told him before, she didn't whore herself out for anyone. But…doing a little subterfuge on Trevor's behalf? Maybe that wasn't out of the question…

He studied her proud profile, waiting to see if she would tell him the truth now, after she'd allowed him back inside her body. Maybe she'd explain her reasons for deceiving him.

But she didn't.

Her silence was a punch-in-the-gut reminder of who she was—who they were to each other. She said she wanted to forget. But they never could. Especially when forgetting for even a moment meant letting his guard down and the enemy in.

And that's who she was.

The enemy.

Thirteen

Shay shrugged into her suit jacket, studying herself in her room's cheval mirror. The slim fit of the gray, pin-striped jacket and pencil skirt were flattering, emphasizing the curves of her waist and hips. The cream blouse with the throat-to-waist ruffle lent it a feminine flair. She'd gathered her hair into a loose bun and fastened a pair of her mother's favorite diamond studs to her ears. The whole look was professional, fashionable…

And armor.

Yes, she needed it today. Hopefully, no one looking at her would guess that the previous night she'd had hot, wild sex in the back seat of a car.

God. She closed her eyes, pinching the bridge of her nose. What had she been thinking? But that was just it. She hadn't been.

Groaning, she turned from the mirror. It would've been so easy to stay in bed today and burrow under the covers. Just pretend last night hadn't happened. After all, that was her forte lately. Pretend to be in a relationship. Pretend to be in love with Gideon Knight. Pretend she hadn't just thrown all common sense and family loyalty out the window and screwed the man who was blackmailing her.

Regret weighed down her chest, so she couldn't inhale without feeling its bulk. Not regret about the sex. It had been as cataclysmic as the first time, and though it'd been foolish to give in to him, she didn't have remorse over experiencing passion.

No, it was what happened after that earned her regret. For a time, she'd forgotten that Gideon hated everything and everyone associated with the Neal name. That he planned on taking down her brother if she didn't capitulate to blackmail. That they stood on opposite sides of a Hatfield-and-McCoy-esque feud.

But as soon as the pleasure ebbed from her body, he'd returned to his aloof, distant self. She'd practically felt the wall slamming up between them. He'd been gentle when he'd shifted her off his lap and adjusted her dress, but unlike the hands that had cupped her breasts, tangled in her hair and stroked between her legs, his touch had been cold, almost clinical.

Other than asking if she was okay and wishing her good-night when he'd dropped her off at home, he hadn't spoken. And she'd never felt so vulnerable, so… alone. Not even after the night of the blackout.

And to think she'd been so close to telling him she was Camille. That would've gone over well. Not.

Well, lesson learned. Last night was a mistake she wouldn't repeat. She refused to let herself be vulnerable to him again. Get through the next six months. That was her goal. Protect Trevor from Gideon, come into her trust fund, then leave RemingtonNeal to concentrate on her own business.

The days of being under the thumb of the men in her life would come to an end.

To achieve the dream of independence, she could endure six more months of Gideon Knight.

With a sigh, she glanced at the clock on her bedside table. Well, no time for breakfast, and she could grab coffee at the office. If traffic cooperated, she would just make her nine o'clock meeting with the event planners for RemingtonNeal's huge annual holiday party.

Grabbing her coat and purse, she descended the steps, her mind already locked on the multiplying items on her to-do list today.

"Shay."

She halted at the front door, shooting Trevor a hurried smile as she set her purse on the foyer table to slip into her coat.

"Morning, Trevor. I'm sorry I don't have time for breakfast. I have a—"

"You'll need to make the time. I need to talk with you immediately. And it's too important to put off. I'll meet you in the study." He didn't wait for her agreement, but pivoted on his heel and strode toward the rear of the house.

Bemused, she stared after him. Removing her arm from her coat sleeve, she tossed the garment over her purse and followed her brother.

"Shut the door, please," he said, when she entered the room he considered his domain. As their father had done before him.

Trevor hadn't changed much in the room. Except for the dark chocolate office chair that sat behind the massive oak-and-glass desk, everything else was the same. The tall bookshelves that lined two of the walls, the heavy floor-to-ceiling drapes, the two armchairs flanking the big fireplace. She'd hated being called into this room when her father had been alive; it'd meant she'd somehow screwed up. And she didn't like it any better now with her brother.

"What's going on, Trevor?" she asked, crossing her arms over her chest. Another thing she hated. Feeling defensive.

"Why did I have to find out about you and Gideon Knight from Madison and her father?" he snapped, stalking around his desk. "Do you know how humiliating that was for me, receiving that phone call?"

Of course. How could she have forgotten about Madison and the senator?

Gideon, that's how. Gideon and sex in the back seat of his car.

"I'm sorry, Trevor," she said, truly remorseful. She'd fully intended to tell him about her and Gideon's "relationship" when she arrived home last night, but it'd slipped her mind. "I wanted you to hear about us from me first."

"Us?" he sneered, his hands closing on the back of the chair several feet from her. "There shouldn't even be an *us*. I told you to stay away from him," he reminded her with a narrowed glare. "Do you remember? It was when you told me you barely knew him and there was nothing going on between you two."

"Like I told Madison last night, the fund-raiser wasn't the place to discuss my personal life. Especially when you didn't try to hide your hostility toward him. I've been seeing Gideon for a while now, but because of who we are, we decided not to make our relationship public until we knew we were serious about it." Great. Now she was lying about her lie. "But like I also told the senator, I don't need to run my relationships by you for permission. I did intend to give you the *courtesy* of telling you about Gideon last night. So again, I apologize if you were embarrassed discovering it from someone else."

"Where's your loyalty, Shay?" he hissed. "Your duty to family first?"

Pain struck her like a fiery dart to the breast. It spread through her until she vibrated with it. Reason whispered that he didn't know all she sacrificed—was still sacrificing—for him. But it didn't halt the hurt from his condemnation, his disgust.

"My loyalty is always to this family," she whispered. "Who I'm seeing socially should have nothing to do with you or my love for you."

"It does if you're screwing a man I hate. Have always hated," he snarled.

"Why?" she asked, lowering her arms and risking

a step forward, closer to him. "Tell me why. Gideon told me you went to school together."

That hadn't been all he'd said, but even as shameful and horrible as her brother bullying him was, surely there had to be more to the story. Especially on Trevor's end. Yes, he was a snob, but she'd never seen him actively hate someone just because they came from humble beginnings.

"Yes, we went to school together, and he didn't know his place back then, either."

"Didn't know his place," she repeated slowly, not believing that he'd uttered those ugly, bigoted words. Yes, they were fortunate enough to be in that elevated percentage of wealthy Americans. But they were still black. They still endured racists who gave them the "you're not our kind, dear" looks when they dared enter some establishments. How dare *he*…

"Why? Because he's Chinese-American?" she rasped.

"No." He slashed a hand through the air. "I don't give a damn about that." The vise squeezing her chest eased a little, and relief coursed through her. "After Mom died, all I had left was Dad."

Oh God. "Trevor," she said, moving forward, holding a hand out toward him.

"No," he repeated, coupling it with another hand slash. "I know you were there, but she was something different to me than to you. She was the shield, the… insulation between him and me. When she died, she left me exposed to him. To his expectations, his impossibly high standards, his disapproval. I didn't get time to grieve for her because I had Dad riding my ass, wanting to make a real Neal man out of me without my mother's babying. His words," he added, his tone as caustic as acid.

"I know," Shay murmured. "I saw how hard he was on you. But, Trevor?" She lifted her hands, palms up. "What did that have to do with Gideon? Dad didn't know Gideon."

"But he did," Trevor snarled. "Who do you think funded the scholarship that enabled Gideon to attend the prep school? One of RemingtonNeal's charities. And Dad never let me forget it. Sports, academics, even the damn debate team—Gideon and I were always head-to-head in everything, and when he beat me, Dad was always right there to remind me that a poor scholarship kid was better than me. That maybe he should hire him to run the family company because he was smarter, stronger, quicker, more clever. He constantly compared us, and it didn't end with high school, but continued in college and beyond, even following Gideon's career after he graduated. The one thing I'm grateful for is that he's not alive today to see you with him. He probably would claim him as his son, give him RemingtonNeal."

Shock pummeled her. She'd had no clue. But now his animosity toward Gideon made sense, because she knew her father. Knew how denigrating and belittling and cruel he could be. Especially toward Trevor. Lincoln Neal probably didn't even like Gideon, but using him as an emotional weapon against his son sounded like something he would do.

And Trevor... God, if her brother didn't let go of his bitterness, he would live trying to prove to their dead father that he was better than a man he might have counted as a friend once upon a time.

"Do you understand why you can't be with him, Shay? That man has been the source of my pain and unhappiness for over a decade. I won't allow him in my home or to eat at my table, much less date my sister." He shook his head. "End it."

I can't.

The words bounced off her skull, pounded in her chest. To call off her relationship with Gideon would be to destroy her brother. But even in an alternate universe where she and Gideon had met under normal circumstances without blackmail and revenge, she still wouldn't have broken up with him based on what her brother had shared. Trevor's antagonism for Gideon wasn't his fault—it was their father's. But with Lincoln Neal gone, Trevor had transferred all his resentment and pain to the one who was still alive.

"No, I won't end it with Gideon," she said. Sighing, she moved across the small distance separating them and covered his hand. "Trevor, I—"

He jerked away from her, taking several steps back and glaring at her. A muscle ticked along his clenched jaw. "You won't break this *thing* off with him?"

"No, Trevor, I won't." *I'm doing this for you*, she silently screamed. But the words remained trapped in her throat.

"I didn't want to do this, but you've left me with no other choice. Leida Investments, Shay."

For the second time in the space of minutes, shock robbed her of speech. Icy fingers of astonishment and dread trailed down her spine.

Trevor cocked his head to the side. "You believed I didn't know about your little company all this time? Nothing gets by me. And as long as you were discreet, I didn't see the harm in letting you dabble in business. It didn't interfere with your responsibilities to this family. But now, your actions are jeopardizing us. If you don't end it with Gideon, I'll ruin every business that has received money from you. And with my name and reputation, you know I could do it with just a whisper. Now, while you take some time to make your decision about who you're giving your loyalty to, I'm going to insist you step back from your job at RemingtonNeal. I've already asked Madison to take over some of your duties for the next few weeks. Consider it a leave of absence while you choose between a man you barely know and your family."

With that parting shot, he exited the room, not pausing to spare her a glance. Not even bothering to glimpse the devastation he'd left behind.

Not only had he dismissed her easily, replacing her with his fiancée, but he'd threatened her company, as well as the hard work and livelihoods of those she'd invested in.

He would cavalierly ruin others' lives to bring her to heel.

Forcing her feet to move, she left the study and re-traced her steps to her room. There, she removed her suit and went to her closet for her suitcases. Forty minutes later, she once more descended the stairs, not knowing when she would return.

She couldn't stay here any longer.

Not when she wasn't sure who she was selling her soul to protect.

Fourteen

Gideon pulled up in front of the small brick house in the Humboldt Park neighborhood. With its white trim, meticulously manicured front lawn and currently empty flower boxes, the home was cute and obviously well taken care of.

But Shay still had no business being here.

Not when she had a home.

So why had she sent him a text informing him he'd need to pick her up here tonight, as she would be living in this place for the foreseeable future?

What the hell was going on?

The questions had burned in his head, then twisted his gut into knots. The need for answers had propelled him out of his mother's house, where he'd been visiting her and Olivia. He hadn't bothered replying to

Shay's text but had entered the address in his GPS and driven directly there.

He shut off his car and walked up the tidy sidewalk to the postage-stamp-size porch. Maybe she'd heard him arrive, because before he could knock on the storm door, Shay appeared in the entrance, wrapped in a cashmere shawl and evening gown. She joined him on the porch, scanning his attire, her gaze running over his peacoat, down his black jeans to his boots, then back up.

"You're going to the ballet dressed like that?" she asked, frowning.

"No," he answered shortly. "Come on."

He'd offered her his hand before considering the gesture. They weren't in public, so the display of affection wasn't necessary. But when she wrapped her fingers around his, he only tightened his hold. And didn't think about why he did it.

Moments later, with her safe in the passenger's seat, the full skirt of her gown tucked around her legs, he started the car and drove away.

"What's going on, Shay?" he asked. "Whose house is that?"

"My best friend, Bridgette. You met her that day in the food truck," she replied, keeping her gaze straight ahead.

Impatient, Gideon pressed, "And? Why are you staying with her—how did you put it—for the foreseeable future?"

She sighed, and he steeled himself against the punch

of that tired sound. "Because I left home. And I don't know when, or if, I'll return."

Surprise winged through him, and quick on its heels was fury. Cold, bright fury. "Did you leave or did Trevor kick you out?"

Another sigh, and when he glanced over at her she shook her head. "I left. We…had a disagreement, and I thought it best if I gave us both space."

"You're trying to make me drag it out of you, aren't you?" he growled.

"I'm not trying to make you do anything," she said, every inch of the society princess in that reply. "What's more, I don't *want* you to."

His fingers curled around the steering wheel, his hold so tight the leather creaked. Part of him longed to jerk the car over three lanes to the side of the road and demand she confess everything to him, because he knew there was more to the story. And from those sighs and the tension in her slender frame, he sensed the "disagreement" with Trevor hadn't been pretty. It'd hurt her. And for that Gideon wished he could strangle the man.

But the other part… That part longed to pull over, too, but for a different reason. It wanted to park, release her seat belt and tug her onto his lap so he could hold her. Comfort her. Murmur into her ear that everything would be all right, that *she* would be all right.

Which was ridiculous. If there was a woman who didn't need comforting—didn't need *him*—it was Shay Neal.

Quiet settled in the car like a third passenger as he

drove to his home. It wasn't until he pulled into the underground parking garage that she stirred.

"I can wait here or in the lobby while you change if you're not going to be long. The ballet starts in about thirty minutes," she said, straightening in the passenger's seat.

"Don't be ridiculous," he snapped, her obvious reluctance to be alone with him irritating him. Did she expect him to jump her? "I promise to keep my hands and dick to myself. Now can you please get out of the damn car?"

He didn't wait for her answer, but shoved the door open. But he still caught her grumbled, "Speaking of dicks…"

In spite of the anger and frustration churning in his chest, he couldn't suppress the quirk of his mouth. This woman gave as good as she got.

Minutes later, they entered his penthouse, and as he took her wrap to hang up, lust joined the cluster of emotions he was feeling. While the champagne-colored skirt of her dress flowed around her legs, the top clung to her shoulders, arms and torso—except for the deep V that dipped between her breasts and even lower in back. He briefly closed his eyes, turning away from the alluring sight of her. Immediately, images of the night in his Town Car skated over the back of his lids like a movie trailer. Him, cupping those breasts, drawing them into his mouth…

Cursing under his breath, he jerked open the closet door and, with more force than necessary, hung up her shawl and his coat.

How could she flaunt sex and sophistication at the same time?

"Would you like a glass of wine? Scotch?" he asked, stalking into the living room and toward the bar.

"Do we have time for that? If you don't hurry and dress, we're going to be late," she reminded him, following him, but halting on the top of the steps that led into the living room.

He removed the top of a crystal decanter and poured himself a finger of bourbon. Only after he'd downed a sip did he turn and face her. Staring at her golden skin and the inner curves of her breasts, he took another. He needed the fortification.

"We're not going to the ballet," he informed her.

She frowned. "What? Why not?" She stepped down into the room. "And why didn't you tell me you changed your mind at Bridgette's house?"

"Why?" he repeated, lifting the tumbler to his lips and staring at her over the rim as he sipped. "Because even though you won't admit it, you're hurting. Something more than a 'disagreement' had to have occurred to make you leave the only family you have left, as well as the only home you've known. I'm a self-confessed asshole, Shay, but even I wouldn't make you attend a social event and fake a happiness you're far from feeling. Especially when your brother might be in attendance." He swirled the amber liquor in his glass and arched an eyebrow. "And as for why I didn't tell you when I picked you up, that's simple. You wouldn't have come with me if I had. The last thing you need right now is to be alone. And since I know your friend supplements her food truck income with a part-time job, you would've been very much alone tonight. So that leaves me."

Her frown deepened. "It's a little creepy how you know so much about me and everyone I'm close to."

He shrugged, taking another taste of the bourbon. "Before going into battle, it's wise to be prepared and know everything you can about your enemy."

"Enemy," she breathed, then scoffed. "You just proved my point. We're not friends—far from it. So why do you care how I spend my night? I'm not your responsibility," she said softly.

"No," he agreed just as softly. "We're not friends. But can we call a truce and resume hostilities tomorrow?" He risked drawing nearer to her. "You're right, you're not my responsibility. But I am responsible. The argument was about me, wasn't it?" When she didn't reply, he gently pressed, "Shay?"

"Yes," she reluctantly admitted.

"Let me guess," he said, his anger rekindling. "Trevor wanted you to break it off with me and you refused."

"Correct again." She notched her chin up at a defiant angle, but he caught the slight tremble of her bottom lip. "But if I'd given in to his demand, then it would've meant destroying everything he cares about, destroying him. Still, it's not like I could share that with him. Instead, he threatened to dismantle my company, starting with ruining all the businesses I've invested in. Oh, and he fired me—or placed me on a temporary leave of absence. So those are my choices. End our relationship and destroy everything my brother loves. Or continue upholding our bargain and lose the company I love."

Fury blasted through him, and for a moment a red haze dropped over his vision. Trevor had threatened his own sister? Gideon grasped the tumbler so tightly the beveled edges dug into his flesh. He pictured that thick, brown file in his office safe, and had no regrets about his intentions to expose Trevor. A man like him deserved the hell Gideon planned to rain down on him.

"I won't let him do that," Gideon promised. Soon enough her brother would be too busy trying to pick up the flaming pieces of his life to worry about harming her company.

"It's not your concern." She waved a hand, dismissing his vow and the topic. "And you mentioned a truce? I accept." Moving forward, she extended her arm. "Should we shake on it?"

Gideon glanced down at her open palm before lifting his gaze to meet her eyes. Though his mind ordered him not to touch her, he wrapped his hand around hers. For several long moments, they stared at each other. An electric shock ran through him at lightning speed and jolted his body to attention. It would be an impossibility to be skin-to-skin with her and not respond. But he didn't pull her closer, didn't try to seduce with his words.

Space and sanctuary, that's what he'd promised her.

"Are you hungry?" he asked, lowering his arm to his side. "I can order in anything you'd like."

"I..." She hesitated, shrugged a shoulder and

started again. "I can cook if you have something in the kitchen."

Since meeting Shay, he'd been surprised so many times, he should really stop being taken aback by her. But once more, she'd done the unexpected.

"You can cook?" Dubious, he scanned her beautiful hair, gown and shoes. "In that?"

She snorted. "You're not starting off this truce thing well. And yes, I can cook." If he hadn't been watching her so closely, he might've missed the flash of insecurity that was there and gone in an instant. "Show me to the kitchen? That is, if you don't mind me...?"

"No, this I have to see for myself," he assured her, and strode past her toward the room he rarely used. His housekeeper often prepared dinners for him that she left warming in the stove. So the pantry and refrigerator should both be stocked. "I'll even supply you with clothes so you don't get anything on your dress. See how accommodating I am?"

"Until tomorrow," she added from behind him.

"Until tomorrow," he agreed.

"I wouldn't have believed it if I hadn't tasted it for myself," Gideon exclaimed with wonder, staring down at his empty plate.

Shay shook her head, smothering a smile, although her cheeks hurt with the effort. Forking the last of the chicken carbonara to her mouth, she tried not to blush under his admiring scrutiny. She was twenty-five and an heiress—needless to say, she was used to compliments. But coming from this man... She returned her gaze to her plate, not wanting to analyze why it was different.

"Can I say something without breaking the tenuous bonds of our truce?" he asked, cocking his head to the side.

She wanted to duck her head and avoid his piercing contemplation. It cut deep. Exposing her. Even with the distance of the breakfast bar separating them, she had the sudden urge to lean back, insert more space between them.

But she remained seated and met his gaze. "Sure."

"I would've never pegged you for someone who enjoyed getting their hands dirty in a kitchen. I know you helped your friend out that day in the food truck, but I thought that was a fluke. What you did in there—" he dipped his head in the direction of the kitchen "—was skill. And spoke of someone who really enjoyed it. You're a walking contradiction."

"So your all-knowing file didn't include that information?" she mocked. Picking up her wineglass, she sipped the moscato, silently debating how much to tell him. Then, before she could make up her mind, her mouth was moving. "My mother loved to cook. We had a personal chef, but when Dad wasn't home, she'd commandeer the kitchen and cook for all of us. She would let me help, and some of my happiest memories are of the two of us preparing a pot of gumbo or baking a quiche. I learned to cook from her, but I also inherited my love of it from her."

God, where had all that come from? Embarrassment rose in her, swift and hot.

"Anyway, now your dossier is complete," she added flippantly. "I'll clean up."

She rose from her chair and, grabbing both their plates, circled the bar and headed toward the sink. As she set the dishes in it, a long-fingered hand settled over hers, stilling her movements.

"She would've been proud of you," Gideon murmured in her ear. Heat from his body pressed into her side, her shoulder. "Now, go relax. You did all the work, the least I can do is clean up."

Her first instinct with Gideon was always to defy his orders. She wasn't a puppy. But this time, she accepted his offer and slid from between him and the counter.

Coward.

Maybe.

Okay, definitely. But his unexpected displays of tenderness and the potent, dark sexuality that he emitted like pheromones combined to undermine every guard she'd erected since that night he'd so coldly rejected her after giving her devastating pleasure.

She went in search of the restroom, and after locating it and washing her hands, she continued her tour of his place. At least the downstairs. A formal dining room. A bedroom done in soft blues and cream. Maybe this was where his sister, Olivia, slept when she came over; he'd said the T-shirt and leggings he'd given Shay were hers. Until that moment, she hadn't even known he had a sister. But he didn't offer more information, and for the sake of their temporary cease-fire, she didn't ask.

Another bathroom. A study. A den.

She paused at the open door of that last room. With its two couches, love seat, numerous end tables, large coffee table, massive television screen mounted above the fireplace, this space appeared more lived-in than the rest of the penthouse.

She glanced behind her, but the hallway remained empty. *Just a peek*, she promised herself, then she'd leave. Moving into the room, she stroked a hand over the leather couch that bore a distinct imprint in the middle cushion.

Must be where Gideon sat the most. She could easily imagine the man she'd spent this evening with—in his black, long-sleeved, V-neck sweater, black jeans and bare feet—relaxing in this room. Feet up on the table, remote in hand, scanning through the no-doubt-numerous channels before deciding on…what? Funny. She knew how he had sex, but had no clue about his favorite TV shows or movies.

For some reason, that struck her as sad.

It also lit a hunger to discover more about him. Some things they'd shared in the blackout, but not nearly enough to satisfy her curiosity. What was his favorite color? His favorite band? Snack? Boo—

Oh God.

Breath trapped in her throat, she crossed the room toward the instrument that had captured her attention. No, *instruments*. Plural. A glossy black stand with padded interior cradled six guitars. She knew nothing of guitars, but she could tell the three acoustic and three thinner, sleeker electric guitars had to be expensive. And obviously well cared for.

A flutter tickled her stomach, launching into a full-out quake. She reached a slightly trembling hand toward the guitars.

"Do you play?"

She whipped around, guilt snaking through her. "I—I'm sorry," she stammered, backing away from the instruments. Damn, she was a sneak. And not even a good one. "I didn't mean to snoop, I…" She paused and inhaled a deep breath. "I was taking a self-guided tour of your house and saw the guitars. They're beautiful," she whispered. "I don't play, but obviously, you do…?"

He nodded, crossed the room on silent bare feet and halted next to the stand.

"For years," he said, brushing an affectionate stroke over the gleaming wood of an acoustic guitar. Her thighs tightened, the touch reminding her of how he'd caressed her skin. A lover's familiar caress. "We didn't have a lot of money when I was growing up. But when I showed an interest and aptitude for guitar, my mother somehow managed to scrape enough together for lessons. I didn't find out until I was a teenager, but my father played the guitar, too. I don't remember it, but I like to think I inherited my love of music from him, as you did cooking from your mother."

"Will you—" She broke off. God, she was pushing her luck. From his explanation, she sensed he didn't share this part of himself with many people. It didn't line up with the image of ruthless business tycoon. But in this moment, she wanted to see his clever, talented fingers fly over those strings. To witness him coax beautiful music from that instrument. To watch him lower that damnable shield and let her in. "Will you play for me?"

He stared at her, and her heart thudded against her rib cage. Finally, *finally*, he dipped his chin and reached for the acoustic guitar on the far end. He almost reverently lifted it off the stand and carried it to the love seat. She trailed behind him, not saying anything. Afraid if she uttered a word, he might change his mind. Once he perched on one end of the small love seat, she sank to the other.

Propping the instrument on his thighs, he plucked a few strings, turned the knobs at the top. Once he seemed satisfied, he cupped the neck, fingers at the ready there. And the other hand hovered over the big, rounded body.

Then he started to play.

And...*Jesus*.

She'd expected something classical, reserved. But no. Passion flowed from beneath his fingers. Passion, and anger, and joy and grief. So many emotions soared from the music, which sounded almost Spanish, but bluesy and a little bit of rock. It was fierce, soul-jarring and...and beautiful. So. Beautiful.

Pain swelled in her lungs, and she expelled a huge breath, just realizing she'd been holding it.

When his fingers stilled, and the music faded away, she remained speechless, breathless. Like she'd been transported to Oz and offered this rare peek behind the wizard's curtain. Only she didn't find a fraud, but a rare, wonderful truth about this man. One that few people were gifted with seeing.

He lifted his head, and those fathomless black eyes studied her. A faint frown creased his brow, and he reached for her, swiping his thumb under her eye.

"You're crying," he murmured.

"Am I?" she asked, shocked, wiping her fingers over her cheeks. Well, hell. She was. "I didn't notice."

"Was I that bad?" he teased, with a soft smile she'd never witnessed on him.

"You were—" *are* "—amazing," she whispered. "Thank you for sharing that with me."

The smile disappeared, but his midnight gaze glittered as if dozens of stars lay behind the black.

"I shouldn't want you." She blurted out the confession. "I shouldn't. But… Even knowing who we are… Even knowing this can only end one way, I still want to grab on to those moments when we're just Gideon and Shay, not someone's enemy or sister. When we're being honest with each other the only way we truly can."

Sex. Need. Passion—they're honest. The body can't lie. Lust is the great equalizer regardless of social status, race or tax bracket.

It was a risk saying those words to him, since he'd uttered them to Camille, not her. And from the gleam in his hooded gaze and the tightening of his sensual mouth, maybe he remembered giving them to another woman.

Honesty. Though her pulse slammed her ears, she had to drag her big-girl panties on and tell him the truth. She couldn't justify keeping it from him anymore, especially when he'd offered her the gift of playing for her.

"There's something you should know," she murmured. "I've been keeping something from you. The night of the blackout, Bridgette had come down with a bad cold and asked me to take her place at a job so she wouldn't lose it. Gideon, that was at the Du—"

"Shay, I already figured it out. You're Camille."

Her lips parted with a gasp. She blinked, staring at him. How had he…?

"Did you really believe I could be inside your body and not remember?" he murmured. "Not remember every detail of how tight and sweet you are? No, moonbeam." He shook his head. "I'd never forget that."

"Wait." It suddenly made sense now. His rejection afterward. "Is that why you were so cold to me? Because I hadn't told you?"

He studied her for a long, quiet moment. "It wasn't so much that you lied, but wondering *why* you were at the gala and why you kept the truth from me."

"Bridgette would've lost her job if she'd called in on such short notice, and with her business just getting off the ground, she can't afford that. And I had to use a disguise and a fake name. I've attended the gala in the past, and my brother also…" She trailed off, a dark inkling beginning to stir in her head. "My brother," she whispered. "Did you think I'd been there because of him? That I sought you out for him?"

After a slight hesitation, he nodded. "The thought occurred to me."

"Someone must have hurt you terribly for you

to be so mistrusting and suspicious," she continued softly. And she had an idea about the identity of that "someone."

"Trevor had no clue I was there. There were only two people in that break room, Gideon—you and me. What happened between us was the scariest and most exhilarating, *freeing* thing I've ever done. That's what you make me feel. Terrified out of my mind because no one has ever affected me so viscerally I don't recognize myself. While at the same time, I'm excited because I like it…crave it."

As soon as the confession escaped her, she recognized that he could use it to his advantage. But she mentally shook her head. Gideon wasn't like her brother. He might utilize blackmail to gain her compliance, but never once had he tried to use her passion against her. He might be ruthless, but he possessed his own code of honor.

Sex. Desire. It was their Switzerland.

And she'd seek asylum there for a while before they found themselves on opposite sides of a war again. Because that was inevitable.

But for now…

She shifted closer to him, covered the hand that still rested on the body of the guitar. Lightly, she explored those fingers, amazed at how they could draw such magic out of the instrument and her. She wanted him to cradle, strum and play her.

She trailed a caress up his arm, over his shoulder and neck, until she reached his jaw. Cupping it, she mimicked the many times he'd held her in the same grip. She swept her thumb over his full bottom lip.

His gaze never leaving hers, Gideon carefully set the guitar on the table, then clasped her hand in his. He turned his head, placing a kiss in the center of her palm, then tracing a path to her wrist. His lips pressed there over her pulse, and her lashes fluttered down. But at the damp flick of his tongue, she gasped, eyes flying open. Liquid heat pooled between her legs, and she didn't even try to contain her whimper.

He rose, gently tugging her to her feet. Without releasing her hand, he led her out of the room, down the hallway and up the curving staircase. They entered a cavernous bedroom lit only by a single lamp on a nightstand. Not just any bedroom—his. The big king-size bed covered in a black spread and white pillows, two chairs flanking a large, freestanding fireplace, a couple glossy bedside tables, a rug—the almost austere decor was relieved by the breathtaking view of the Chicago River and city skyline through the three floor-to-ceiling windows, and the one wall that bore a black-and-white mural of a bare, leafless tree on a lonely plain. It was gorgeous. It was him.

Turning to her, he captured all her attention by cradling her face between his palms, tilting her head back and claiming her mouth. Slow, tender; raw and erotic. His tongue relayed all that he wanted to do to her—would do to her. And as she cocked her head to the side, granting him deeper access, she consented to it all.

"I've had you on a couch and in the back seat of my

car. I want to take you on a bed," he muttered against her lips. "*My* bed."

As soon as her whispered "Please," passed her lips, he stripped her, haphazardly tossing her borrowed clothes to the floor. His clothes followed and, hiking her in his arms, he carried her to the bed. Her back hit the covers and his big, hot body pressed her into the mattress. He kissed her harder, wilder, more insistently, as if that leash on his control had unraveled. She dug her fingers into his hair, yanking off the band that corralled it and freeing the strands so they tumbled around both their faces. With a hot, low rumble, he kissed her again, then every inch of her received attention from his mouth, his fingers. By the time he tugged open the drawer on a bedside table and pulled a condom free, she shook with need, twisting and aching for him to fulfill his promise and take her.

Linking their fingers, he drew her arms up, their joined hands bracketing her head.

"Open for me, moonbeam," he murmured, desire burning hot in his dark eyes. The head of his erection nudged her entrance, and she willingly, eagerly widened her thighs and locked them around his slim hips. "Thank you, baby."

He groaned as he sank inside her, not stopping until her sex fully sheathed him. She arched under him, grinding her head into the pillow. God, he stretched her, filled her. Branded her. When he started to move in long, hard thrusts that rocked her body and her soul, she felt claimed. And when her channel clenched around him, and she hurtled into an orgasm that threatened to break her apart, she shut her eyes and became a willing sacrifice to it.

Soon, the aftershocks rippling through her eased, and the fog of ecstasy started to fade. She tensed, waiting for him to roll away from her, to reject her. But when he drew her into his arms, his still-labored breathing bathing her neck, she slowly relaxed.

Right before she drifted away, his low, hoarse voice penetrated her heavy blanket of drowsiness.

"Don't let me break you, Shay. Protect yourself from me."

She didn't reply, but carried that warning with her into sleep.

Fifteen

Shay nabbed the slice of bread out of the toaster and spread avocado on it. She ate it leaning against the counter, alternating between sips of fresh coffee. Gideon had already left for the office, and with a glance at her wrist, she realized she didn't have long before she had to leave, too. Since she no longer had a position at RemingtonNeal, she'd scheduled a meeting with a potential client.

Staying the night hadn't been in the plan. But when he'd curled around her after he'd made her body sing its own special melody, she hadn't wanted to go anywhere. And then he'd woken her with a cup of steaming coffee, keys to one of his cars and a sweet but wicked kiss that left her toes curling into the mattress.

But those lovely gestures couldn't completely erase

the kernel of apprehension that lingered at the edge of her consciousness.

Don't let me break you, Shay. Protect yourself from me.

His murmured warning stayed with her, and dread wormed its way through the warmth. He didn't caution her to be careful because he might hurt her, but because he would. And she would be foolish to ignore that truth. Real life was blackmail, revenge, vendettas and pain. Only in fairy tales did frogs turn to princes. Or wolves to heroes.

Cold seeped into her veins. Suddenly losing her appetite, she dumped the remains of her breakfast. She needed to get going and return to the real world outside this penthouse.

She was heading toward the closet to collect her wrap and dress when the front door opened. Startled, Shay stared as a woman who looked to be about her age entered. With wavy black hair that tumbled over her shoulders, smooth, unlined skin and a tall, slender frame wrapped in a camel cashmere coat, she was obviously too young to be the housekeeper Gideon mentioned last night. Jealousy, unbidden and bright, flared in Shay's chest. Whoever she was, she must be close to Gideon to have a key to his penthouse.

But then the other woman lifted her head, and the truth slammed into Shay. With those heavily lashed, beautiful onyx eyes, she had to be related to Gideon. And considering her age, she was most likely his sister.

"Oh, hi," Olivia said, arching a dark eyebrow in a manner so similar to Gideon's, it confirmed her identity. "I'm sorry. I didn't know Gideon had company. I can come back."

"No, you're fine," Shay objected, finding her voice as his sister half turned to grasp the doorknob. "Gideon's not home, and I was just leaving, too. You must be Olivia." Shay moved forward, her hand extended. Gideon's sister stepped away from the door with a smile, her arm lifting. "My name's Shay. Shay Neal."

Olivia froze, except for the arm falling woodenly back to her side. "Neal?" she repeated in a tremulous whisper. "Are you related to Trevor Neal?"

Unease crawled through her. "Yes. Do you know him?"

Olivia paled, her eyes widening. Visibly trembling fingers lifted to her lips and pressed against them. "I didn't—no, he wouldn't—"

Her fractured sentences made little sense to Shay, but the woman's obvious distress amplified the dread until it was full-out fear. "Olivia, are you okay?" she asked, risking moving closer.

Olivia jerked her head from side to side, tears glistening in her eyes. "Why are you here?"

"Gideon and I are…" She paused, unsure of how much to expose. "…seeing each other. Would you like to sit down? Can I get you anything?"

Again, Olivia shook her head, the tears streaming down her cheeks now. Unable to stand the woman's pain, Shay reached for her, wrapping her in a hug. She half expected Olivia to shove her away, but instead, the woman clung to her, sobbing now.

God. Shay tightened her embrace, her own eyes

stinging. What kind of agony must Olivia be in to cause this kind of reaction? It burrowed inside Shay, and she wanted to soothe it, to take it from her. Gently, she guided the crying woman to the living room and lowered them both to the couch. She continued to hold Olivia, gently rocking her as her mother used to do when Shay ran to her in need of comfort.

She didn't glance at her watch to see how long they sat there. If Olivia needed her to remain the whole day, she would. Anything so those awful, tearing sobs would stop. Gradually, Olivia calmed, and only when she went silent and the trembles eased did Shay slip her arms away. Her shoulders twinged, but she ignored the slight ache. She left for the bathroom. Minutes later, after a quick stop in the kitchen, she returned with a box of tissues, a warm, damp cloth and a bottle of water.

"Thank you," Olivia whispered, her voice hoarse from her tears. "I—I'm sorry. I didn't mean to—"

"Please don't apologize. It's okay," Shay assured her. The woman's clear air of fragility stirred a sense of protectiveness in Shay. "I'm a stranger to you, and you don't have to talk if you don't want to, but I'm here. And whatever you say will stay between us."

For several moments, Olivia clutched the bottle between her hands. Though she'd wiped her face with the cloth, her eyes remained stark, her cheeks and lips pale. Shay waited, ready to listen if Olivia chose to confide in her, ready to just sit with her if she decided not to.

"I know your brother," Olivia finally said, haltingly

at first. "I met him a year ago, and we…we fell in love. Or at least I did. I don't know if he ever did love me. But he told me so. And I believed him. I would've done anything for him—and I did. He asked me to keep our relationship a secret because he and Gideon were business rivals, and he didn't want any of that interfering with us. I'd heard Gideon mention Trevor before and knew he had no love for him, so I agreed. Also, I figured once he saw how much we loved each other, he would come around. Especially since I became pregnant."

Shay gasped, unable to contain her shock and dismay. At the sound, Olivia lifted her gaze from the water bottle. The grief and unadulterated pain there shook Shay, and she wanted to gather the other woman in her arms again. But she didn't, sensing Olivia needed to get this out, like lacerating a festering wound so it could heal faster.

"I thought he would be happy about the news. I was overjoyed. All I dreamed about was marrying him and starting a family. We would be doing it a little out of order, but I didn't care. But—but…" She paused, and a sob escaped her.

Shay grabbed her hand, offering her support, and Olivia went on. "When I told him about the pregnancy, he told me he didn't want me or the baby. To get rid of it because I was no longer useful to him. Then he walked away, like I was garbage he'd tossed out the window. He used me to get back at my brother. At the time, I worked at Gideon's company as his executive assistant. I was so naive, so snowed by Trevor, that when he asked me questions about Gideon's agenda, who he was meeting with, I gave him the information. He worded it to make it sound like he was only asking about my day, what I had on my plate, but he was pumping me for inside information. He never loved me, never had any intention of creating a family with me." She shook her head, her throat working, as if swallowing back another sob. "I refused to end the pregnancy, but it didn't matter. I miscarried and lost the baby."

Shay remained sitting next to Olivia, but inside she reeled, enraged screams slamming against her skull. Part of her longed to deny the story, to label Olivia a liar, but she couldn't. Not only could she not violate this woman all over again by not believing her, but deep inside her soul where only honesty existed, she knew Olivia wasn't lying. Her utter agony bore witness to it, and Shay believed her.

Grief assaulted Shay, welling up in her, and she silently wept. For Olivia. For her pain. For Shay's own pain. For Trevor's coldness, controlling behavior and dismissal of her hopes, dreams and needs. For her disillusionment about her brother. If Trevor could treat his own sister so callously as well as do something as despicable as take advantage of this woman for personal gain, then what else was he capable of? Maybe those things in Gideon's dossier?

Gideon. Was Olivia the reason behind his plans? The night in the restaurant, when he'd first showed her the incriminating file, he'd scoffed at her claim that Trevor wouldn't care who she was dating.

Oh yes. Your brother will care. And he'll understand.

Then, his assertion had been cryptic, but now, understanding dawned on her. No wonder he hated Trevor and had no qualms about blackmailing her. This was more than a business deal; Trevor had come after Gideon's family. If she'd harbored any fledgling hope after waking up in his bed this morning that maybe they could have something more than a truce, this knowledge obliterated it. She would always be a living reminder of the harm and damage her brother had inflicted on his sister, his family.

There was no forgiveness for that. Not for her brother.

And not for her, being guilty by association.

Sixteen

"I still don't think this is a wise decision."

Shay stared out the rear window of Gideon's Town Car at the Gold Coast historic mansion lit up with a cheerful glow. A steady stream of people climbed the front stone steps of the place she'd called home for nearly twenty-six years, entering for Trevor and Madison's engagement party.

"You and Trevor might not be seeing eye to eye right now, but I'm sure he wouldn't want to celebrate his engagement without his sister," Gideon said from beside her.

She glanced at him, irritation and something deeper, sadder pressing against her breastbone like a large boulder. "You won't pass up an opportunity to turn the screw, will you?"

With his aloof mask firmly in place, he met her gaze, onyx eyes steady and unblinking. "No."

She faced the window again, that heaviness gaining weight. It'd been a week since she'd walked out of her childhood home. A week since her and Gideon's truce, which had stretched longer than the next morning. A week since she'd held Olivia as the woman broke down in her arms and revealed Trevor's betrayal.

Yes, now Shay understood the motives behind Gideon's blackmail. And a part of her couldn't blame him. But another part—the part that remembered the man who'd played guitar for her, the man who'd cuddled her close in his bed after tearing her apart with pleasure—longed for him to put all of this aside.

For her.

To want her more than revenge.

She shut her eyes, making sure to keep her head turned away so he couldn't glimpse the yearning that she was certain leaked into her expression. In spite of knowing it was the epitome of foolishness, she'd started to fall for Gideon.

No, that was a lie. The fall had started some time ago, at what moment, she couldn't pinpoint. Maybe when he'd revealed his own pain to her in the back seat of the car. Maybe when he'd raced to Bridgette's house and decided to place her comfort above putting on another episode of the Gideon and Shay Show at the ballet. Maybe when he'd sat on that couch with his guitar and revealed a part of himself that he didn't with most people.

Not that narrowing down the exact instant mattered.

The truth was she loved Gideon Knight.

His fierceness. His heart, which he tried to hide. His passion. His love for his family.

Yes, he was a hard man, a merciless man, but never a cruel one. And when she looked at him, gazed into those midnight-and-stars eyes, she dreamed. She stupidly dreamed that he could love her as he'd once adored Madison before she'd scarred him with her disloyalty and infidelity.

Maybe she did believe in fairy tales, after all.

The door to the car opened, and with a sigh, she climbed out, murmuring a thank-you to the valet who stood next to it. Seconds later, Gideon's body heat warmed her back, and his palm settled at the base of her spine. A spine she straightened.

No time for self-pity now.

She had the performance of a lifetime to give.

Because she was walking into the lion's den knowing her arrival on Gideon's arm would announce her decision to her brother—she'd chosen his enemy over family loyalty. That's how Trevor would see it.

And she wasn't naive; there would be consequences to her decision. No job at RemingtonNeal. She would most likely have to find a place to live because she couldn't stay with Bridgette forever. And, most importantly, Leida Investments and the businesses she'd invested in would be affected. Especially if Trevor followed through on his threat of tampering with the start-ups she'd funded. She had savings, and she could use most of it to provide capital. But the possibility of having to scale back or rebuild her company was very real without her salary.

The cost of loving Gideon was high.

And, God help her, she was willing to pay it.

Gideon walked silently beside her, but the tension rolled off him, and it ratcheted higher when they entered her home and handed their coats to a waiting servant.

She seamlessly fell back into the role of Chicago socialite and, pasting on a smile, mingled with the other guests. Many of whom didn't seem surprised to see her with Gideon, so the gossip about them as a couple must've made the rounds. Still, they were aware of the enmity between Gideon and Trevor as business rivals, and watched her and Gideon with an avid, greedy curiosity.

Especially when a path seemed to open, and they stood only feet away from Trevor, Madison and Senator Reus. Shay looked up, and her gaze connected with her brother's. Though he smiled for the benefit of those around them, fury blazed from his hazel eyes, so like hers. His glare shifted from her to Gideon, and a frightening rage hardened his expression before he controlled it.

"Stand tall, moonbeam," Gideon murmured in her ear. His big palm slid up her back and under her hair, curling around the nape of her neck. "He can't hurt you."

But you can. The words rang in her head, her chest. Tipping her head back, she said, "That's debatable. Cutting me off emotionally and financially and targeting my company definitely falls under the 'hurting me' category."

"Correction, then," he growled. "I won't let him hurt you."

That ship had sailed and was a faint glimmer on the horizon.

She straightened her shoulders and added a little more wattage to her smile. "We should go greet the happy couple."

"You mean, get it over with?" he retorted, dark eyebrow arched. She'd once detested the gesture, but now counted each one.

"That's what I said."

His low chuckle tripped over her bare arms. Inhaling a deep breath, she allowed him to guide her over to the trio who stoically watched their approach.

"Trevor, Madison, congratulations." She leaned forward and stiffly kissed Madison's cheek. Although she did return the feigned embrace, most likely for those closely observing them, Madison's rigid posture didn't relax. Straightening, Shay nodded to her brother's future father-in-law. "Senator."

"Shay," he murmured coldly.

"Your sister wanted to see you, wish you well," Gideon said to Trevor, his tone frigid, but she detected the undercurrent of anger. Of hatred. "She has a forgiving heart considering you put her out of her own house."

Oh God.

"She left by her own choice," Trevor snapped, the fury in his eyes leaking into his face. His lips twisted into an ugly snarl. "But come now, Gideon. We both know how trying *sisters* can be."

Nausea churned in her belly and raced for the back of her throat.

Dark waves of rage poured off Gideon, and he moved forward. Terrified, she latched on to his arm, fearful of what he might do to her brother. And she feared *for* Gideon, for the consequences he might suffer for his actions. She harbored no doubt that Trevor would enjoy pressing charges and using it against him.

"Gideon, no," she pleaded softly. "It's what he wants."

Trevor sneered. "Shay, I need to speak to you. Alone," he stressed.

"Fine," she agreed, more to separate Gideon from Trevor than to be amenable. "Gideon," she whispered. When he tore his still-frightening stare from her brother, she squeezed his arm. "I'll be right back."

"You don't have to do this," he reminded her, just as softly, but the fury still vibrated in his voice.

"Yes, I do," she returned. Rising onto her toes, she placed a kiss on his jaw. "They're not worth it." She waited for his abrupt nod before she turned back to her brother. "In the study, I assume."

Not waiting for his confirmation, she strode toward the rear of the house. Anger bristled under her skin, poking her like thousands of tiny needles. When she entered her brother's domain, she could barely look at him.

"How dare you bring that asshole into my house?"

Trevor ground out through clenched teeth as soon as he closed the study door behind them.

"Your house?" She crossed her arms. "You were right when you told Gideon that I chose to leave. Chose. Because this is *our* home, Trevor. I can bring whoever I want here, and you have no say. I don't need to ask your permission."

"I would've never thought you were a traitor," he snarled. "Mom and Dad wouldn't recognize you right now."

She absorbed the power of that blow and fought not to stagger from it. But the pain ebbed and flowed inside her.

Stand tall. He can't hurt you.

Inhaling a deep breath, she pushed past it.

"You're such a hypocrite," she said, surprised at her even tone. "So righteous and high-and-mighty. And to think I defended you. Believed in you. Trusted you. But you didn't deserve any of it."

"What the hell are you talking about, Shay?" he demanded. "I've done nothing but honor this family, the Neal name, *you*. You, baby sister, betrayed me."

"By thinking for myself, wanting something for myself? For daring to defy you? I'm not a sheep, Trevor. I have a mind. I have feelings. I have a heart, but there's only one Neal who can claim to possess the last two. Because somewhere along the way, you lost them to jealousy, pettiness and hate. No, *big brother*," she said, throwing his taunt back at him. "I've done nothing but stand by this family. I've protected it when you would've destroyed it with your greed and ambition."

"You need to stop right there," he warned in a dark growl, taking a step forward.

But he didn't intimidate her. Didn't control her. Not anymore. She didn't wait for him to advance, but marched forward and met him halfway.

"No, you stop. And listen. I know what you and your precious senator are up to," she said. "Insider information. Fixing contracts. Kickbacks. Illegal campaign contributions. And that's just the tip of it." When he rocked back in shock, his eyes flaring wide, she nodded. "Yes, Trevor, I know about it all. Because Gideon has a file on you, inches thick. I've seen it, read it. I'm aware of all your dirty dealings, which if made public could topple RemingtonNeal, ruin the Neal name and send you and Julian to jail."

"How long have you…?" His voice trailed off, but she understood his question.

"Weeks. Since before the Grace Sanctuary fundraiser. I made a deal with the devil to save you. I agreed to pretend to be in a fake relationship with him so he wouldn't expose you. That's why I couldn't break things off with him. Because if I did, you would've been destroyed. But that's not all," she whispered, eliminating the small space between her and the man who wore her brother's face, but was a stranger. "He did all this because of Olivia. You remember her, don't you?" At his stony expression, she nodded again. "Of course you do. The woman you seduced, used to get back at her brother, impregnated, then tossed aside. All for your petty hatred and resentment. Now, who wouldn't Dad and Mom recognize?"

"You don't understand," he spat, but the anger in his eyes had been overshadowed by worry. By fear. Because he understood that his greatest enemy had the dirt on him, no doubt. "You could never understand…"

"Not understand what? How hard it is to live up to our name? To live under the yoke of it for so long that sometimes you feel like your back's going to break from the burden? Yes, Trevor, I do. The difference between you and me is that I'm choosing not to let it poison me until I make unconscionable decisions that hurt other people. I decided to help people rather than harm them. But just to get your way, you would steal that from me, too."

For too long, she'd allowed him and the duty of being a Neal to dictate her life, her behavior, her decisions. No longer. She might have been quiet, but she'd learned from the best.

Not him. Gideon.

"I love you, Trevor. For the brother and man you were, I'm giving you a choice now. Come after Leida Investments or any of the businesses I've invested in, or my trust fund, and Gideon won't have to leak any of that information to the press and SEC. I will. He gave me a copy of the file, and right now, it's tucked away safe. But if you dare touch anything that's mine—and when I say mine, that includes Gideon Knight and everything he loves—I'll take you down. And I won't lose sleep over it."

Trevor stared at her, shocked. But she didn't wait for his response. He couldn't say anything that would fix what he'd broken. She would just have to accept that some men changed for the worse instead of the better, and as much as it tore her heart apart, Trevor was one of them.

"I have to admit, Gideon, I never expected you to go to *these* lengths." Madison tsked, appearing at his side, her familiar scent teasing his nostrils.

At one time, he'd found the floral fragrance alluring. Now it was just cloying. She trailed fingertips down his arm and over the back of his hand. Tilting her head to the side, she offered him what she probably considered a coy smile. She didn't pull it off. Not when he knew the real woman behind the mask.

He shifted his arm, knocking her hand away. Foolish as hell of him to think he could slip unseen into the closed-off room that reminded him of his den. He'd needed space and time to walk off the killing rage that had consumed him when Trevor had alluded to Olivia.

If not for Shay, he would've put that bastard through the wall, his hands around his throat, and damn the consequences. But his name in that soft voice and the fear darkening her lovely eyes had stopped him. He'd put that hated emotion in her gaze, and he detested himself for it. Still, even with rage roiling inside him like a volcano set to blow, he would've accompanied her to that meeting with her brother. He hadn't wanted to leave her alone. That protective streak toward her had only widened and deepened in the time they'd spent together. Yet he also understood she needed to have it out with Trevor, to stand up to him on her own.

And she couldn't do that with his life in imminent danger from Gideon.

But right after he marched into an empty room to cool off with a glass of bourbon from the bar, Madison had appeared.

Goddamn, he didn't have the patience to deal with her machinations right now.

"What lengths, Madison?" He lifted the tumbler to his lips, downing the last of the dark alcohol before setting the glass on the mantel. "I don't have time for your games."

"Time for me," she corrected, assuming a hurt expression. "That's what went wrong with us, you know? You spent so much time at the office or out of town at meetings, I felt neglected. I missed you and couldn't stand the loneliness."

He snorted. "Is this your way of trying to explain why I walked in on you sitting on Trevor's dick? Forget it, sweetheart. This guilt trip not only isn't going to work, but it's months too late. I don't give a fuck now."

"We both know that's not true, Gideon," she crooned, clutching his arm. He stiffened, hating her hands on him. It felt…wrong. There'd been a time when he'd enjoyed her teasing caresses, her heated strokes. But now? Now his skin prickled and crawled as if his very body rebelled against her. These days, he welcomed the touch of only one woman. Shay.

Again he shifted away, dislodging her touch.

"If you'd answered any of my phone calls this week, you'd know—"

"I didn't answer them because we have nothing to talk about," he said.

"So you're going to tell me that your love for me just died? Went away just like that?" She snapped her fingers, eyes flashing. "I don't believe it."

"Believe it," he growled. "You killed it. And you don't get a do-over. Get it through your head, sweetheart. I. Don't. Want. You."

Tired of this, he went to move around her, but she sidestepped, blocking him. Unless he wanted to grab her, pick her up and shift her out of the way, he couldn't pass. And at the moment, the thought of putting his hands on her caused his stomach to curdle.

"Then what was this whole…act with Shay about? You don't expect me, or anyone for that matter, to actually accept that you're madly in love with her? The sister of the man who stole the woman you love? You don't have to continue this silly pretense anymore, Gideon." She shoved into his personal space, so her perfume clogged his nose, crawled down his throat. He grabbed her shoulders to prevent her from coming any nearer. She flattened her palms on his chest. "I love you. I made a mistake leaving you for him. It's been you all along. And I know you still love me if you'll go to these lengths."

Screw this. He tightened his grip on her, prepared to move her. "Madison…" he growled.

"Yes, Gideon." She moaned, and shooting up on her toes, wrapped her arms around his neck and crushed her mouth to his.

Shock froze him. But just for a second. Bile scorched

a path to the back of his throat. Muttering a curse, he jerked his head back, circled her wrists and yanked her off him.

"Dammit," he snapped. But any more words died on his tongue.

Shay stood in the doorway to the den, her shuttered gaze on them.

"Oh, Shay," Madison cooed, panting lightly. "We didn't see you there." Perverse satisfaction threaded her tone.

"Shay," he breathed, already leaving the unfaithful bitch he'd almost married behind, forgotten, and moving toward the woman with the wounded eyes.

"I'm ready if you are," she said, her voice flat, hideously polite.

She turned on her heel and left, leaving a void in his gut.

Seventeen

Shay stared out the window of the Town Car, watching the landmarks that defined Chicago passing by in the distance. What she wouldn't give to be in one of those monuments right now. Just anywhere as long as it wasn't here, sitting in the back of this car, tension thick, her pain crushing her chest like an anvil.

Tonight had been a special hell. Between the confrontation and probable loss of her relationship with Trevor and walking in on Madison and Gideon kissing, she just wanted to hole up somewhere and wait out this pain. But how could she hide from it, when she embodied it, breathed it?

Next to her, Gideon was silent, brooding. She'd never seen him brood. Distant, yes. Taunting, yes. Passionate, God yes. But never this dark heaviness that seemed to reach out to her, wrap around her.

Hold on, she reminded herself. Just hold on until she could get out of the car and into her temporary home, where she could break down. But not now. Not in front of Gideon.

"Shay."

His deep, silken voice stroked over her skin even under her coat, and she flinched away from it.

"I didn't kiss her, Shay," he rasped.

She squeezed her eyes shut. As if she could block out the sight of Madison, her arms thrown around him, her mouth pressed to the one that she adored, needed. But that image would no doubt be branded onto her brain for all eternity. As well as the slashing pain on her heart.

Yet… "I know, Gideon."

A pause, and then an audible exhale. "You believe me," he stated.

She nodded. "Yes."

"Then, baby, look at me. Please." It was the "please" that had her turning her head and meeting that midnight gaze. "Then what's wrong? Why haven't you spoken to me, looked at me since leaving the party? Tell me what I've done and let me explain it."

"You haven't done anything," she said, scanning his features. Committing them to memory. "But I can't go through with this charade. Our agreement is over."

His head snapped back, his eyes narrowing on her face. "Why? Did your brother convince you to leave me?"

"Leave you?" She chuckled, and it grated her throat

raw. "You once accused me of being blind, Gideon. It seems to be contagious. You can't see that I would do anything to stay with you. But not as a pretend girlfriend or a lover-for-now. I want the real thing. I *deserve* the real thing."

"Shay," he said, and her heart squeezed so hard, she placed her hand over her chest. "What are you saying?"

"I'm saying I love you. Desperately. Completely. Finally. There's no going back for me. There's no one else. And that's a problem, because you don't love me. You don't want me other than as a bed partner and a means to an end."

"That's not fair," he rumbled, the skin tautening over his cheekbones, anger diamond-bright in his eyes. "You mean more to me than a fuck. I've never treated you like that. I never would."

"No," she agreed. "You've been one of the few men in my life who saw past the socialite, the family name and money. You saw the business owner, the capable woman. When no one else respected me, you did... even as you used me to get back at my brother. And that's the problem. Because above all, the first thing you will always see is Trevor Neal's sister." She hesitated, but in the end, she had nothing to lose in laying it all out there. "I know about what he did to Olivia," she said.

Gideon transformed into living stone. Except for his eyes, which blazed with anger and another darker, more heartbreaking emotion.

"How did you find out? Surely *Trevor*," he spat her brother's name, "didn't confess his sins to you."

"No." She shook her head, hurting for him, for Olivia. Shame for Trevor's despicable actions coating her in grime even though she wasn't responsible for him. "I didn't tell you, but Olivia came by the morning after I moved out of my house. She broke down when she realized who I was, and she ended up revealing everything to me. She's the reason behind the file, the blackmail, the revenge, not Madison. Your hatred goes much deeper than him cheating with her."

"Yes," he confirmed, still cold, still impenetrable. "You saw for yourself what he did to Olivia. She's been emotionally fragile ever since he left her, and she lost the baby. The morning after the blackout, she'd found out about his engagement to Madison. And it sent her to the hospital. She's recovering, but she hasn't been the girl I remember since before your brother came along."

"And you'll never be able to get past that. Not that I blame you. He crossed an unforgivable line, and there's nothing that could justify it. But even realizing this, I can't waste one more day hoping you will let it go. Not one more day living a lie. It's time for me to live for me, to determine and shape my own future, and I can't do that with a man who insists on remaining in the past. A man for whom revenge is more important than love…than me."

"I didn't ask for your love," he snapped, and the tone, razor sharp, flayed her already wounded and bleeding heart. "I told you not to let me break you, Shay. I warned you."

"And I didn't ask for your permission to love you,"

she countered softly. "Don't feel guilty, Gideon. I'm used to not being enough for the men in my life. But the difference—what you've taught me—is I no longer give a damn. I'm enough for *me*."

At that moment, the car stopped in front of Bridgette's house. Shay didn't wait for the driver to come around and open her door. She unlocked it and did the honors herself. It was like a metaphor for her new life. She was tired of waiting on others. She was in control of her own fate; she could open her own doors.

And she would.

Starting now.

"Shay." Gideon's strong fingers grasped her wrist. "Please."

"Goodbye, Gideon," she whispered.

Then, pulling free, she stepped out of the car.

And didn't look back.

Eighteen

Gideon entered the numbers into the spreadsheet, then several seconds later swore under his breath and deleted them. *Dammit*. He'd been doing a repeat of this same thing for hours now.

Hours, hell. His fingers fisted on top of the keyboard. Days.

His concentration had been shot for five nights and six days. Since the five nights and six days ago when Shay got out of his car. When she'd announced she loved him, then walked away without looking back. As an image of her leaving him, spine ramrod straight, glide elegant and proud, wavered in his head, he squeezed his eyes shut. Bowing his head, he didn't will the mental picture away. No, he conjured it up over and over, punishing himself with the memory of the pain and soul-deep sadness that had darkened her eyes, of the words that had driven daggers into his chest.

Of the resolve and strength radiating from her that let him know if he didn't say something, *do* something to prevent her from exiting the car, he would never see her again. Never inhale her rain-and-roses scent. Never hear her husky voice. Never have her body pressed to his, fitting like a missing puzzle piece.

But he'd done nothing.

That grab at her wrist had been weak, and they'd both known it.

"Damn you, Shay," he whispered harshly. "Damn you."

Like he'd told her that night, he hadn't asked for her love. Didn't want it. He'd earned a PhD in how faithless love was. People threw that word around to abuse, betray and abandon others. Madison had claimed to love him. Trevor had vowed the same to his sister.

Love deceived, used and…died. It left pain and disillusionment and loss behind. It changed people for the worse, not the better. Intuition had warned him that if he allowed Shay in, if he risked opening to her, when she left—because experience had taught him the leaving was inevitable—the wreckage would be much worse than the damage Madison had inflicted. Shay would level him.

He refused to be played for the fool by *love* again. Ever.

With that "ever" ricocheting off his skull, he turned back to his computer screen and the report he'd been trying to finish for the past two hours.

His desk phone buzzed. "Mr. Knight, there's a Mr. Trevor Neal here to see you. He doesn't have an appointment—"

"Send him in," Gideon snapped.

What the hell was Trevor doing here? Scratch that. He didn't give a damn.

For the first two days after dropping Shay off, Gideon had tried to drown her out with alcohol. When that had failed, work had been his next attempt to erase her from his mind. Apparently, that wasn't succeeding, either. While meeting with Trevor was most likely a terrible idea, he was also spoiling for a fight. A grim smile stretched across his mouth. For the first time in days—six days and five nights, to be exact—he looked forward to something.

Seconds later, his office door opened, and the man he'd resented for thirteen years and actively hated since he'd harmed Olivia stalked inside. Harsh lines etched his forehead and bracketed his mouth, and his eyes, so like his sister's, blazed with anger. His hands curled into fists at his sides. Seemed like Gideon wasn't the only one looking for a fight.

His smile widened.

"Good afternoon, Trevor. I'd say it was nice to see you again, but we both know that would be bullshit. So we'll skip the pleasantries and get to what are you doing here." Gideon leaned back in his desk chair and templed his fingers beneath his chin.

"You son of a bitch," Trevor snarled.

"Well, that didn't take long," Gideon drawled with a sigh, his voice heavy with mock disappointment.

Rising, he flattened his palms on the top of his desk. "What the fuck do you want?"

"Where's my sister?" Trevor demanded. "I checked with Bridgette. She's no longer staying there. So where is she?"

"I don't know," Gideon replied calmly. Though inside, alarm clanged in his head, his chest. As far as he'd known, she'd still been with her best friend. *Was she okay? Was she safe?* The questions barraged him, but he forced his focus back to the man across from him. "Why do you care? You let her leave the only home she ever knew because she wouldn't bend to your demands. Are you suddenly having an attack of conscience?"

Doubtful, since the man didn't have one.

"Not that it's any of your business, but I need to speak to her. Last time we spoke, she made some… irrational accusations and threats. We need to clear this up. As a *family*," he sneered.

Gideon arched an eyebrow. "Threats?" Pride and admiration warmed him. "There's an interesting turn of events."

"You would find it funny." Trevor scowled. "She wasn't like this before. I'm thinking it's the company she's been keeping."

"Thank you." Gideon dipped his head in acknowledgment. "And just for the record, your sister has always been strong. You were just too busy playing lord of the manor to recognize it. If you had, maybe you would've used her brilliance for the advantage of your *family* company instead of sticking her in some bullshit position. Then she might not have had to go form her own business, but could've helped yours grow."

"You know nothing about Shay," Trevor growled, shifting forward as if ready to leap over the desk. "Don't pretend that your *relationship*," he spat the word, "was real. She told me the truth about your blackmailing her into pretending you two were a couple. She also informed me about the file of lies you have on me."

Shock reverberated through him. When she'd claimed she wouldn't go one more day living a lie, had she been referring to confessing to her brother about their arrangement?

Flipping these new revelations over and over in his mind, Gideon returned his attention to Trevor. "You might have tried that argument with Shay, but don't bother with me. Everything listed in that file is the least of your crimes. We both know who you are, Trevor. We both know what you're capable of," he growled. "You used my sister, then tossed her aside like she was something beneath your shoe. No, I take that back. You would've at least paused and scraped something off the bottom of your precious loafers. You didn't even give her that courtesy. And for what? A grudge against me from high school? You broke her, and for you it was business as usual."

"Like you broke my sister?" Trevor accused. "Eye for an eye? Don't stand there and preach to me like you're so self-righteous, when you turned around and did the same thing to Shay. You used her to get back at me. That doesn't make you the hero in this story."

"You're right."

Trevor's mouth snapped closed, his eyes flaring in surprise at Gideon's quick agreement, before narrowing. He was probably wondering what Gideon's game was now. But there wasn't any game. There wasn't any trickery to slide another point home as if this was a contest to be won.

He'd used Shay. Oh yes, he'd justified it as righting a wrong against Olivia, as protecting future women from being hurt by Trevor. But the truth couldn't be denied any longer. His actions hadn't been noble— they'd been selfish, vengeful…and reprehensible. Maybe unforgivable.

Not because of Trevor. He still had zero fucks to give about Trevor. But because he'd dragged an innocent into it. As blameless as Olivia had been in Trevor's schemes, Shay had been just as blameless. His mother's warning haunted him, ringing in his head like a premonition that had come to pass. He *had* ended up hurting others. And the most important person he'd hurt was Shay. No, he wasn't Trevor—could never deliberately deceive and devastate someone, then walk away from a child he'd created—but he'd also blackmailed, hurt, then turned his back on the woman he loved.

God. He loved her.

The force of the revelation struck him with the blow of a mallet to the chest. He sank to his chair, staring blindly ahead.

He loved Shay.

Somehow, despite every wall, every barrier and

shield he'd thrown up, she'd wedged herself into his heart, his soul. No wonder he'd felt so empty these past days. The one who'd given him life again was gone. Because, yes, she'd resuscitated him, jolting his heart so it beat again. She'd given him more than work to be excited about—she'd given him her quiet humor, her defiance, her wit, her loyalty, her body...her love.

And what had he done? Thrown it back at her like it meant nothing.

Don't feel guilty, Gideon. I'm used to not being enough for the men in my life.

Pain, razor sharp and searing hot, razed his chest. He gasped at the agony of it. Nothing—absolutely nothing—could be further from the truth. She was more than enough. She was *everything*. But he'd been willing to throw away a future with her for revenge.

"Gideon," Trevor snapped, hauling Gideon out of the hell he'd plummeted into.

He jerked his head up, blinking. God, he'd forgotten all about this man standing in his office. And now he didn't have time for him or the vendetta that had brought both of them low. Urgency spiraling through him, Gideon shot to his feet and strode across the room. Removing a large picture from the wall, he revealed the safe behind it and quickly punched in the code to open it. He withdrew the thick, brown file inside, then slammed the safe door shut, not bothering to replace the painting.

"Here." He marched over to Trevor and shoved the dossier containing all his damning information into the other man's chest. "Take it. There aren't any more copies other than the one I gave your sister."

"What?" Trevor gasped. He clutched the folder, glancing at it before his gaze whipped back to Gideon. "What's your angle now? You can't seriously just hand this over to me without wanting something in return."

Gideon stepped back, shaking his head. "No angle. No ulterior motive. But you're right. I do want something in return. Or rather, someone. I want Shay. More than that file or revenge against you. But that's for me to fix, not you."

How he'd go about doing that, he had no clue. Hell, by all rights, she shouldn't forgive him. But he needed her. He loved her.

And he'd fight to have her. Harder than he'd ever fought to pay back Trevor.

Because winning Shay was more important than any battle he'd ever faced.

Nineteen

"Order up, babe."

Shay turned around and rushed across the minimal space inside the food truck to grab the two cartons of larb served over thin noodles. Snatching up napkins and plastic utensils, she placed everything in a bag and handed it to the waiting customers through the window. Smiling and thanking them, she turned to the next person and took his order for green papaya salad.

Bridgette had called that morning, asking if she would help her out on the truck again. Though Shay suspected her friend had arranged this sudden lack of help to keep her busy and her mind off a certain person, she'd jumped at the chance to get out of her newly leased, empty Edgewater apartment. More specifically, she'd been eager to get out of her head.

In the almost two weeks since she'd walked away from Gideon, she'd found an apartment—despite Bridgette's argument that she could stay with her as long as she wanted—located a small office space for Leida Investments, officially resigned from RemingtonNeal, opened a safe deposit box for the damning file on her brother and done more research on start-up companies that she could invest in.

Yes, her family and love life had exploded, but she refused to stop living. A gaping hole existed where her heart had once been, but that didn't mean she would roll over and give in. She'd meant every word she'd uttered to Gideon.

This was her time. Her life. And no one but she was in control of it.

She might have lost the man she loved because he wanted revenge and hate rather than her, but for the first time in longer than she could remember, she loved herself. She *valued* herself. And she was demanding it from everyone in her life.

As Bridgette had put it, Shay was a boss.

Dammit, yeah, she was.

She'd learned something in the last couple weeks. She would've loved having Gideon in her life. But he *wasn't* her life.

And she was okay with that.

"Have another order for the larb, but by itself, without the noodles," she called out to Bridgette over her shoulder before returning her attention to the window and the next customer. "Hi, how can I..." She trailed off, the sudden lurch of her heart to her throat preventing the rest of the words from escaping.

No.

No.

She stared into midnight eyes with stars and the scream inside her head increased in volume. It wasn't fair. What the hell was he doing here? Telling him she loved him and having him reject her had been agonizing, humiliating. How did he not know that? Was he a sadist getting pleasure from her pain?

Well, *screw that.*

She schooled her features into the cool, polite mask she'd mastered since she'd been old enough to sit at the adult table. He wouldn't get anything else from her. She didn't have it in her to give.

"What are you doing here, Gideon?" she asked, proud when not so much as a tremor shook her voice.

Behind her, Bridgette appeared next to her elbow like a bodyguard. "What the hell is this?" she demanded, spatula still in hand.

"I got this," Shay murmured to her friend. "We're busy, as you can tell," she said to Gideon. "And you and I don't have anything left to say to each other."

Again, she sounded calm even to her own ears. Sounded as if her fingertips didn't tingle with the need to touch him.

But inside…

Inside she quaked. Love, hurt, yearning, desire—they all coalesced and swirled in her chest, leaving almost no room for air. She dragged in what little she could and waited.

"You don't have to say anything, moonbeam. All I ask is for you to listen."

"Don't call me that," she snapped, and silently cursed herself for betraying that much emotion. She shouldn't care if he murmured that endearment. It shouldn't affect her.

"Two minutes, Shay." His dark gaze searched hers. "Please."

Please.

Like before, it gave her pause.

"Two minutes. That's it," she agreed.

"Thank you," he said, then hesitating, he dragged his hands over his head. Taken aback by the uncharacteristically nervous gesture, Shay narrowed her eyes on him. Noting for the first time the faint smudges under his eyes, the two-minutes-past-five-o'clock shadow that darkened his jaw. Where was the clean-cut, reserved man she'd known?

He gave a rough, abrupt chuckle. "Now that I'm here, I don't know where to begin." Sighing, he dropped his arm. "First, I should apologize. And I am sorry, Shay. I used you. There's no getting around that fact. I rationalized and defended my actions by claiming I wanted justice for Olivia. That your brother had gotten away with hurting people long enough, and if no one else would make him pay, then I would. But what I didn't want to admit is that I blamed myself.

"I hated myself as much as, if not more than, him. It was my job to protect my sister, and I failed. If I'd been a better brother, she would've felt free to tell me about the relationship with Trevor instead of keeping it a secret. And most of all, if not for me, she wouldn't have even been on his radar. Me. It all came back to me, and I couldn't bear the guilt, the shame and, God, yes, the anger. It was that anger that led me to do what I had judged him for—ruthlessly using you to get to him. I convinced myself I was more honorable than him, but in my rage, I'd *become* him. And worst of all, I hurt you. That, I will never forgive myself for."

Soul-deep shock robbed her of speech. Even the long line of people behind him had stopped grumbling and were quiet. A few even had their phones out. She mentally winced. Gideon wouldn't be happy to know he was probably live-streaming on social media.

"Gideon, you don't have to—" she began, only to be cut off.

"Yes, I do. I'm desperate, Shay. I don't have any pride left. Not when it comes to you. And I don't want it. Don't need it. Not when it kept me from telling you how important you are. God, baby, you're *vital*. Nothing is the same without you in my world. Before you, work, family, money, success—those were priorities. Hell, they were everything. But since you walked away from me, I still have all of those, and aside from my mother and sister, they don't fulfill me anymore.

"I can't concentrate at work because I'm wondering where you are, what you're doing…if you're thinking about me. I could escape into all the things wealth buys, I could travel to the most exotic places on this earth, but I'd see nothing, appreciate nothing, because you wouldn't be there with me. Success?" He held up his hands, palms out. "Until you, I measured success by how many clients I had, the profits, how many doors opened for me. But now? Success is how many times I can make you smile. How many times I can hear you say I love you. How many nights I can fall asleep beside you. How many ways I can prove to you that you're loved. So far, I've been damn unsuccessful."

"Wow," Bridgette whispered beside her. Shay shot her friend a look, and she shrugged, smiling sheepishly. "I mean, bastard."

Shaking her head, Shay returned her gaze to the man who'd captured her attention and that of an increasingly growing lunch crowd in Hyde Park. She blinked back the tears stinging her eyes, and her heart pounded thickly against her rib cage. Hope tried to rear its foolish head, but she slapped it back down. She'd been stupid enough to spin impossible dreams around this man once, even though he'd never made promises to her. And that was just it. She could no longer afford to pin nebulous hopes on a man who refused to put her first. No matter how lovely his speech.

"Thank you for the apology, Gideon. I really do appreciate it. But I can't risk taking a chance on you. How long before you realize you're sleeping with the enemy—literally—and resent me for it? I can't live waiting for that day to happen."

"You don't get it, moonbeam," he said, moving closer to the service window. And in spite of her resolve, she leaned forward, a part of her—the part that woke up aching for him every night, the part that refused to stop believing in fairy tales—desperate to hear what she didn't get. "I love you. I don't know when it happened. When I sat down across from you in that restaurant and you essentially told me to go to hell? When you refused to answer my phone call and cater to me because you were helping a friend? When I played my guitar for you? Maybe…" He hesitated, swallowed hard. Then whispered, "Maybe the first time I saw you as Camille."

"Saw you as Camille? What kind of kink are y'all into?" Bridgette muttered from behind her.

Shay ignored her, latched on to every word falling from Gideon's lips. Ensnared by those onyx eyes that she couldn't tear herself away from.

"I don't deserve you. But there's no man on this earth who does. But that won't stop me from fighting for you. From fighting for *us*. From begging you to not throw me away, even though I almost did. Moonbeam, you complete me in a way revenge never could. Without you as my conscience, my lover, my friend, I'm empty. I want to be full. I want to be found. Please, don't leave me out there again. I love you, Shay Neal. Desperately. Completely. Finally. There's no going back for me. There's no one else."

He gifted her with the words she'd given him. Only this time, he was the one standing on the ledge, hoping she would grasp his hand and pull him back to safety, to love. He'd pushed her over that night. And now, she could do the same. Pay him back. Turn away to a future that he wouldn't be in, but would still be good. Or she could reach across, risk her heart again and jump off the edge, trusting him to catch her. And hold her forever.

There was no choice.

Running, she barreled out of the truck, but before she could round it, she crashed into Gideon. He hadn't waited, but met her halfway. That's what they would always do—meet each other. Never fail to be there for one another.

Dimly, she heard a roar of applause and cheers, but as his arms closed around her, and she wrapped hers around his neck, everything else ceased to exist. He captured her mouth in a kiss that stole her breath and sent heat roaring through her. But most of all, it shattered every remnant of fear and doubt, promising her with the thrust of his tongue, the molding of his lips, that he would love her, cherish her, worship her. And she returned the vow.

"I love you," she whispered, peppering his mouth, jaw and chin with kisses. "I love you so much."

"I thought I'd never hear you say that again," he rasped, pressing his forehead to hers.

"I promise you I'll never stop telling you." She took his mouth this time, leaving them shaking against each other. "I love you."

"Forever?"

"Forever."

Epilogue

One Year Later

"Mrs. Knight, your husband's here to see you."

Shay smiled, pressing the speaker button on her desk phone. God, she never tired of being called that. "Please send him in, Jackie." Seconds later, her executive assistant opened the door, grinning as Gideon strode past her. Leida Investments was still small, but now Shay could afford a staff. Even if that staff was just Jackie. Still, the business was steadily growing, and Shay couldn't be happier.

Well, she took that back, her smile warming as Gideon crossed the room and took her into his arms. With the news she'd just received not minutes ago, she could indeed be happier. And she was.

Her lips parted under his, and as always, his kiss kindled the desire that only he could stir within her. She tilted her head back farther, opened her mouth wider, and he dived deeper. By the time he lifted his head, their rough breaths echoed in the office.

"I'm supposed to be taking you to lunch," he reminded her with a sensual smile that was reflected in his eyes. "But with you kissing me like that, hell, moonbeam, you might *be* lunch."

She chuckled. "You're bad. And I refuse to keep your mother and sister waiting. I had to twist Bridgette's arm to let me have Olivia for an afternoon, so nope, not missing lunch."

Gideon's eyes brightened at hearing his sister's name. And no wonder. Olivia had come a long way in a year. After hearing the whole story about what Trevor had done to her, Bridgette had decided to take her under her wing. And Olivia hadn't had much of a choice. Bridgette had bulldozed her way into Olivia's world, and assumed the role of big sister, as Shay had. Soon, she had Olivia in the food truck, working beside her, and to Olivia's surprise, she'd enjoyed it and was wonderful with people and the business side of it. Bridgette had taken her on as a partner, and now the two of them were planning to buy another truck.

And Trevor... A sliver of sadness wormed its way into Shay's happiness. It happened whenever she thought of him. She hadn't shared the file she had on him; he was her brother, and no matter what he'd done, she couldn't destroy him. But things like that had a way of exposing themselves. He and the senator were in trouble with the law and SEC now. Soon,

Trevor would lose not only his wife, the family business and reputation, but also his freedom. He'd caused a lot of pain and loss to people both emotionally and financially, and now he faced the consequences of his actions. She loved him, but she also hadn't seen him since the night of his engagement party.

"Are you sure about lunch?" Gideon asked, cupping her chin and tipping her head back for another press of his lips to hers. "I'm sure Mom and Olivia would understand."

"Yes." Shay laughed, then cradled his cheeks between her palms. "I'm hungry." She paused. "And especially since I'm eating for two now."

Shock blanked his features. Slowly, understanding dawned, and his black eyes glittered.

"What?" he rasped. "Are you telling me that we're… that you're…"

"Pregnant," she finished with a wide grin, slipping her arms around his neck again. "We're going to have a baby."

"Moonbeam," he whispered, awed. With a reverence that brought tears to her eyes, he stepped back, and her arms fell to her sides. He knelt in front of her, his big hands spreading over her still-flat abdomen. "Jesus, Moonbeam. How can you continue making me the happiest, richest, most loved man in the world?" He dipped his head, brushed his mouth over her belly. Rising to his feet, he pulled her into a tight, hard embrace and buried his face in her neck. "I love you, Shay. I love you so much."

"I love you, too. Forever."

* * * * *

What happens in the dark doesn't stay in the dark. Especially for Gideon's best friend and business partner, Grayson Chandler, and the curvaceous beauty who spent the night of the blackout with him. Will he make her an offer she can't refuse?

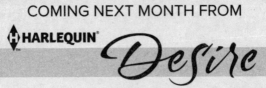

Get 4 FREE REWARDS!

We'll send you 2 FREE Books plus 2 FREE Mystery Gifts.

Harlequin® Desire books feature heroes who have it all: wealth, status, incredible good looks... everything but the right woman.

FREE
Value Over
$20

YES! Please send me 2 FREE Harlequin® Desire novels and my 2 FREE gifts (gifts are worth about $10 retail). After receiving them, if I don't wish to receive any more books, I can return the shipping statement marked "cancel." If I don't cancel, I will receive 6 brand-new novels every month and be billed just $4.55 per book in the U.S. or $5.24 per book in Canada. That's a savings of at least 13% off the cover price! It's quite a bargain! Shipping and handling is just 50¢ per book in the U.S. and $1.25 per book in Canada.* I understand that accepting the 2 free books and gifts places me under no obligation to buy anything. I can always return a shipment and cancel at any time. The free books and gifts are mine to keep no matter what I decide.

225/326 HDN GNND

Name (please print)

Address   Apt. #

City   State/Province   Zip/Postal Code

Mail to the Reader Service:
IN U.S.A.: P.O. Box 1341, Buffalo, NY 14240-8531
IN CANADA: P.O. Box 603, Fort Erie, Ontario L2A 5X3

Want to try 2 free books from another series! Call 1-800-873-8635 or visit www.ReaderService.com.

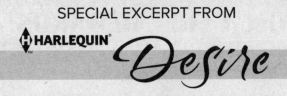
"I don't believe you want to talk about yoga." She lifted
dark, inquisitive eyebrows. "You look like you have
something interesting to talk about."

The pull toward her was real and raw—the realest thing
he'd felt in a while.

"I didn't plan on talking about it…" he admitted, but she
must have heard the ellipsis at the end of that sentence.

She tilted her head, a sage interested in whatever he
said next. Wavy dark brown hair surrounded a cherubic
heart-shaped face, her deep brown eyes at once tender
and inviting. How had he not noticed before? She was
alarmingly beautiful.

"I'm sorry." Her palm landed on his forearm. "I'm
prying. You don't have to say anything."

"There are aspects of my life I was certain of a month
and a half ago," he said, idly stroking her hand with his

thumb. "I was certain that my parents' names were William and Marion Duncan." He offered a sad smile as Hayden's eyebrows dipped in confusion. "I suppose they technically still are my parents, but they're also not. I'm adopted."

Her plush mouth pulled into a soft frown, but she didn't interrupt.

"I recently learned that the agency—" or more accurately, the kidnappers "—lied about my birth parents. Turns out they're alive. And I have a brother." He paused before clarifying, "A twin brother."

Hayden's lashes fluttered. "Wow."

"Fraternal, but he's a good-looking bastard. I just need… I need…" Dropping his head in his hands, he trailed off, muttering to the floor, "Christ, I have no idea what I need."

He felt the couch shift and dip, and then Hayden's hand was on his back, moving in comforting circles.

"I've had my share of family drama, trust me. But nothing like what you're going through. It's okay for you to feel unsure. Lost."

He faced her. This close, he could smell her soft lavender perfume and see the gold flecks in her dark eyes. He hadn't planned on coming here, or on sitting on her couch and spilling his heart out. He and Hayden were friendly, not friends. But her comforting touch on his back, the way her words seemed to soothe the recently broken part of him…

Maybe what Tate needed was her.

What will happen when Tate brings Hayden home for Christmas?

Find out in Christmas Seduction *by Jessica Lemmon. Available October 2019 wherever Harlequin® Desire books and ebooks are sold.*

www.Harlequin.com

Want to give in to temptation with
steamy tales of irresistible desire?

Check out **Harlequin® Presents®,
Harlequin® Desire** and
Harlequin® Kimani™ Romance books!

New books available every month!